BURN THE WORLD DOWN

UNSANCTIONED

BOOK 1

ANNA HACKETT

Burn the World Down

Published by Anna Hackett

Copyright 2025 by Anna Hackett

Cover by Hang Le Designs

Cover image by Ren Saliba

Edits by Tanya Saari

ISBN (ebook): 978-1-923134-88-1

ISBN (paperback): 978-1-923134-89-8

ISBN (special edition paperback): 978-1-923134-90-4

WHAT READERS ARE SAYING ABOUT ANNA'S ACTION ROMANCE

The Powerbroker - Romantic Book of the Year (Ruby) winner 2022

Heart of Eon - Romantic Book of the Year (Ruby) winner 2020

Cyborg - PRISM Award Winner 2019

Unfathomed and Unmapped - Romantic Book of the Year (Ruby) finalists 2018

Unexplored – Romantic Book of the Year (Ruby) Novella Winner 2017

Return to Dark Earth – One of Library Journal's Best E-Original Books for 2015 and two-time SFR Galaxy Awards winner

At Star's End – One of Library Journal's Best E-Original Romances for 2014

The Phoenix Adventures – SFR Galaxy Award Winner for Most Fun New Series and "Why Isn't This a Movie?" Series

Beneath a Trojan Moon – SFR Galaxy Award Winner and RWAus Ella Award Winner

Hell Squad – SFR Galaxy Award for best Post-Apocalypse for Readers who don't like Post-Apocalypse

"Like Indiana Jones meets Star Wars. A treasure hunt with a steamy romance." – SFF Dragon, review of *Among Galactic Ruins*

"Action, danger, aliens, romance – yup, it's another great book from Anna Hackett!" – Book Gannet Reviews, review of *Hell Squad: Marcus*

CHAPTER 1
NASH

"**H**it me." I tapped the felt-covered poker table.

Across from me, my friend, Cole, threw a card down.

I checked it and groaned. "I'm out." In disgust, I tossed the rest of my cards on the table.

"Good," Bastian drawled from beside me. "I'm *definitely* in."

I rolled my eyes and sat back in my chair. Of course he was. Sebastian Thorne was a card shark and won most of our poker games. I wasn't sure why I bothered.

Cole looked unfazed. My gaze swung from him to where Bastian lounged beside me, looking like a king sprawled on his throne, deigning to mix with the commoners.

Cole and Bastian were like a pair of tough biker boots and an expensive set of Italian loafers. Bastian, who owned the fucking casino we were sitting in, wore a stylish shirt in a light-gray color, tucked into tailored suit pants that were no doubt some fancy designer I didn't care about. I guessed women would say Bastian was handsome, since he never lacked for feminine company. He had a hawkish face, high cheekbones, and dark eyes, added to thick, dark hair that was always carelessly styled. He had a constant stream of beautiful women who only ever spent one night in his bed. Bastian had a strict rule: no repeats.

Cole Black, meanwhile, looked like the fighter he was. Broad shoulders, hardpacked muscle, and a rugged face. His nose had been broken before, and he had a wicked scar on his left cheek and neck that could only have come from a knife. He was the kind of guy that made people cross the street when they saw him coming. He looked like he'd chew nails and spit them back at you.

"I'm in, too," another voice drawled.

I arched a brow at the man at the end of the table. Landon rarely played. "You'll lose."

The African-American man shrugged. "I'm feeling lucky."

Landon Bradshaw always had a serious look on his face, like he was contemplating important things. Dark, watchful eyes sat in a strong face, his skin was dark brown, and he kept his black hair short, and his beard neatly trimmed.

"It's your money." I waved at the server hovering nearby. "I'll take another beer."

The young man nodded. "Yes, sir."

We were playing in a private room on one of the upper floors of the Avernus casino. The floor-to-ceiling windows gave us a million-dollar view of the Las Vegas Strip. Outside was filled with glittering, blinking color, beckoning you to come and play, and lose all your money.

Bastian had done well with this investment. The Avernus was one of the newest and hottest casinos on the Strip. It offered the best gambling, the most popular clubs and restaurants, the most-in-demand shows, and had a golf course behind the building.

Only Bastian would use prime Vegas real estate for a golf course.

I accepted my beer and nodded my thanks. I sipped and watched Cole deal more cards. Of course, no one knew that Bastian was the owner of the Avernus. He kept that information well hidden. He'd hired a guy—a handsome actor who'd never moved past playing bit parts in TV shows that only lasted one season—to play the face of the casino.

Being a retired assassin, Bastian didn't like to show his face or attract attention.

Same as me.

I took another sip of beer. All of us at this table had killed for a living. Some in the military, some CIA or MI6, some freelance.

It was a job that eventually cut too much out of the soul. I had zero regrets. I'd gone from Navy SEAL to assassin for my country. I'd put down some of the worst people on the planet. I wouldn't lose sleep over that.

But I'd discovered the military was made up of people and led by people. And sometimes those people weren't good. They were corrupt, more worried about themselves and their own agendas than the greater good.

I shoved those thoughts away. The past was the past.

Nathaniel Hagen, farm boy from Idaho, turned Navy SEAL and military hero, was long gone.

So was the assassin only known as Nightvision. Known for taking out targets with a single shot at night.

Now, I was retired. I was Nash Oakley. I lived in a plush two-bed villa on the golf course of the Avernus casino. Along with a bunch of other retired assassins. Somehow, we'd all found each other.

At first, it had just been me, Bastian, and Landon. The others had slowly turned up and stayed.

I watched Bastian win the game. With a disgruntled noise, Landon threw his cards down.

"I warned you," I said.

"I'll get him next time."

Cole, never a man of many words, snorted. The former freelance assassin started shuffling the cards again.

"Where's Alessio?" I asked.

Bastian shrugged. "Off somewhere on one of his jaunts. You know how he is."

The former Mafia enforcer and assassin had gotten out of the life, but he still ran a few side jobs from time to time.

"And Rafe?" Rafe Archer was the last of our gang.

"I think he's on the Riviera, or the Amalfi," Bastian said.

I shook my head. The former MI6 assassin liked traveling. He also loved art and fast cars. He and Bastian had a competition going for designer suits.

"He should be back at the end of the month," Bastian added.

Landon leaned forward and rapped his knuckles on the table. "I'd better get back to the clinic."

I raised a brow. "It's eleven o'clock at night."

He rose with a powerful move of his hard-packed body. He'd come through the Army, into Delta Force, then into black ops. He didn't talk much about his old work, but I knew it had left its mark.

Landon had gotten out and gotten a medical degree. Now, he healed instead of killed.

He ran a clinic on the Strip that welcomed anyone. Well, except for people Landon deemed on the wrong side of his moral code. He helped the homeless, the not-quite-legal, the poor, the rich. Once, he'd been known as the Blade, but now he used his impressive knife skills on the operating table.

"Night," Landon said. "Catch you later."

Watching him go, I sighed. "I'd better go, too. I'm running a course with the Avernus security team tomorrow." Behind the scenes, I did security consulting for the casinos. Mostly here at the Avernus, but I did a few very quiet jobs for some select casinos. It paid well and it got me out of bed.

Mostly, I didn't care. Mostly I felt tired, empty.

I reached up and rubbed the stubborn tightness in the muscles at the back of my neck. I'd thought leaving the business would be a new start for me. But two years later, I felt…nothing.

I didn't want to go back, and I didn't miss it, but retirement was boring as fuck.

"Some female company might brighten your mood," Bastian suggested. "I know a few ladies who'd be happy to party with you."

I made a sound. "I don't need you to find me a woman."

"Seriously, a decent fuck would help loosen you up."

I growled. "I neither want, nor need, a female parade like you do."

Bastian shrugged. "Your loss." He paused and tilted his head. "I could find you a blonde who looks like that old picture you carry in your wallet."

Shoving to my feet, my chest tight, I shot Bastian the finger. "I'm going to the head."

I stomped to the bathroom, and heard the low mumble of Cole's voice. "Lay off him."

"I'm trying to help," Bastian said.

I shoved the bathroom door open. The inside was as slick and stylish as the rest of the casino. Black, glossy tiles contrasted against the bronze fixtures. Round mirrors glowed with bronze lights. The floor was a mosaic of bronze, gray, and black hexagon tiles.

I stared at myself in the mirror. My brown hair was a little overlong and I probably needed to shave. Bastian's words echoed in my head. I reached into my back pocket and pulled out my wallet. The old, brown leather was worn.

It had been a gift when I was twenty-one from the prettiest girl I'd ever known. I flicked it open and saw the photo.

Georgiana Linden.

My chest rose and fell harshly. My best friend's little sister. I rubbed a finger gently along her smiling face.

Elliot and I had been best friends since we were ten. Back in our small town of Elk Falls in Idaho, we'd been thick as thieves. We'd ridden our bikes all over town, played baseball together, and one time, even stolen a pack of cigarettes and smoked them until we'd been sick. Georgie had been Elliot's sister. I'd never paid her much attention, but hadn't minded the few times she'd tagged along with us. She'd just been Georgie, with her stained jeans and messy hair.

I'm not sure when that had changed, but one day, I'd noticed that the gangly girl had turned into a pretty, young woman. That her jeans hugged gentle curves and her pale-blonde hair looked like starlight. It had been like getting hit by a bolt of lightning.

In the photo, she wore a white sundress, her hair spilling around her shoulders. It wasn't honey colored, but almost white-blonde. It wasn't curly, but wasn't straight, either, but hung in gentle waves. She was smiling at the camera. You couldn't see her freckles in the picture, but I knew they'd be there, sprinkling over her nose. She looked like she should be running along the beach, about to dive into aqua-blue waters.

Elliot and I had joined the Navy together. We'd gone home to visit, not too long after his mom had died. I'd turned twenty-one while we'd been home.

Georgie had given me the wallet as a gift.

And I'd kissed her.

It had been the best kiss in the world.

I rubbed my temple. Then over the next two years, I'd been recruited into a black ops program and Elliot had been killed.

I'd never gone back to Idaho.

My parents had died, and there'd been no reason for me to go back.

Except pretty Georgiana Linden. But by then, I was an assassin gaining a name for myself. And she deserved the best. Georgie deserved a good life in the sunshine.

I couldn't give her that. By then, I'd already had one foot in the darkness, cloaked in gray.

I knew she'd be living the good life. She'd been smart. I knew she'd gone to college because Elliot had told me. I knew she'd have a good job by now, be married to some steady guy. My gut cramped. She'd have a baby on her hip.

Yeah, living the beautiful life.

I closed my wallet. I'd never looked her up. I knew if I saw her, I wouldn't be able to resist the temptation.

Suddenly, several muffled thumps echoed through the wall. My head jerked up.

I knew that sound all too well.

Gunshots.

I shoved out of the restroom.

Cole and Bastian were on their feet, both tense. Bastian had a cellphone to his ear.

"How many?" His voice cut like a blade. "They blacked out the security cameras?" He emitted a low growl and met my gaze. "No, I'll take care of it. Don't call the police. It'll be dealt with. No one fucks with my casino."

He ended the call. "Three men in the High Rollers Suite next door pulled weapons." He tapped his phone screen and pulled up video feed. "They spray-painted the security cameras." A cold smile curled his lips. "But they can't cover the secret ones they can't see."

Cole and I leaned forward.

"How did they get weapons through security?" Cole frowned as he studied the three guys.

The attackers wore black balaclavas. I saw one guy gesturing at the uniformed dealer and the players in the room. The players were all scared, holding their hands in the air. My gaze zeroed in on the weapon the guy was holding.

"The weapons are plastic," I murmured. "Probably 3D-printed."

Bastian's phone pinged with a message from the security team.

"They caught them on security cameras in the elevator before they put their masks on," he said. "They're low-level thieves. Been arrested for hitting some of the seedier casinos."

"Now they're trying to make a name for themselves hitting the bigger places," I said.

A muscle ticked on Bastian's icy face. "You two up for helping me teach these assholes a lesson?"

Cole and I both nodded.

Bastian had saved my life twice—although he maintained it was three times. He could annoy the shit out of me, but he always had my back, and I always had his.

Cole had saved Bastian from a bad situation once, too, back when he'd just been known as the Darkwolf. He could track his prey, silently and relentlessly for days, weeks, months. Whatever it took to take them down.

For better or worse, these men were my brothers.

"Entrances?" I asked.

"They blocked the front door."

"I can get through that," Cole said.

Bastian nodded. "The service entrance at the back leads into a small kitchen and bar."

"That's mine," I said.

"Good. I'll come through the ceiling."

Bastian was former CIA. The guy could sneak in anywhere. Once, he'd been called the Reaper.

He was the last thing you faced before you died.

All of us pulled out our weapons. None of us went anywhere unarmed.

Bastian had a Glock 19.

Cole had a Springfield Hellcat.

I had a custom SIG Sauer P226. I nodded at the others, and we split.

I went to the kitchen, where the server who'd been taking care of us was loitering, looking worried.

"Stay in here and stay down."

The young man's head bobbed rapidly.

A door led into the kitchen of the High Rollers Suite. I quietly opened it, slid through, then closed it behind me.

I heard loud voices and yelling.

"I want everyone's money, phones, jewelry. Everything!"

I waited a beat to give Bastian and Cole time to get into position. The familiar feeling washed over me. A cool focus that flowed through my veins. I felt connected to all my senses. Everything sharpened.

My fingers melded into the grip of my weapon. Making us one.

That should be enough time.

I whirled around the corner and whipped my weapon up.

Before I finished my next breath, I aimed in a fluid move that was second nature and took the shot.

A stocky man with a gun standing closest to me went down.

My next shot was for the man shouting at the front of the room near the dealer. But he was already moving, and I only clipped him. He dove down behind the table.

The man by the door swung around, aiming his gun my way.

I dove and rolled across the black-and-bronze carpet. I came up on one knee, and saw terrified clusters of gamblers.

"Get down," I clipped.

Almost as one, they dropped to the carpet.

Bullets hit the poker table nearby. Bastian would be pissed.

Crash.

I saw Cole burst through the front door. He slammed into the shooter like a linebacker and took him to the floor.

The previous shooter I'd clipped rose, blood on his arm.

"Drop your fucking weapons or I'll kill everyone." He waved his handgun around.

He was so busy shouting, he didn't see the danger drop down from the ceiling panel behind him.

Bastian quietly hit the floor and rose.

Bang.

One shot to the back of the head and the man went down.

I pushed to my feet. "Everyone stay down. The threat is neutralized, and security will be here soon."

I glanced over at Cole who was standing by the door. His target was sprawled on the floor, his head at the wrong angle. Snapped neck.

The security team arrived, rushing through the front door. I nodded at them. They'd been handpicked by Bastian, and trained by me. Security at the Avernus was a well-oiled machine.

I moved to the side with Bastian and Cole. Security hustled the dealer and high rollers out of the room.

Bastian glanced dispassionately at the dead bodies. "Theo."

"Boss?" The head of security stepped over to join us.

"Dispose of them. Where no one will find them."

"Sure thing, boss."

Theo Garrett was older than the three of us, ex-military with some time as a mercenary thrown in. He was a shade under six feet, with a fit, muscular body, and salt-and-pepper hair. He always got the job done, no exceptions.

I suddenly felt bone-tired. "I'm heading home." At least the walk to my villa on the casino grounds didn't take long. Except for Bastian who had the penthouse, all the guys had villas.

Yep, it was like a fucking retirement village for retired assassins.

"Thanks for the help, Nash," Bastian said.

I lifted my chin, then slid my gun into its holster and headed out.

Nope, my life was not sunshine. I knew I wasn't living, I was surviving, but it was all I had.

At least I knew Georgie was living her perfect life.

Then, shoving dreams of things I couldn't have out of my head, I headed out of the casino.

CHAPTER 2
GEORGIE

My life was hell.

I blew out a breath and sank down in a chair at the rickety table. The scent of old cigarette smoke and musty blankets tickled my nose. My hotel room wasn't the seediest place I'd ever stayed, but it was definitely a far-distant cousin to the fancy suites at the swanky casinos on the Strip. This was at the outer fringe of Las Vegas' glitz.

I scraped a hand through my hair, pushing back the drowning sense of despair. God, grief felt like a million razor blades cutting my skin. I still couldn't believe how one day my life was good, and the next, I'd lost everything.

Chest tight, I rubbed my fist against my breastbone. I knew I should get some dinner. But as always, I wasn't hungry. I was never hungry.

You need the strength, Georgie.

For what? I closed my eyes. I had nothing worth living for.

Once, I'd been part of a wonderful family. I'd had

loving parents, a protective older brother, and an annoying younger sister. A sister I could gossip with, argue with, tease.

We'd lived in an idyllic, small town. I'd had life at my feet. I was going to go to college; I was going to get a corporate job. I'd be part of some high-flying, executive team, and wear cool suits.

God, that naïve girl felt a million miles away. Pushing myself upright, I walked over to the mini fridge and grabbed a Diet Coke. I cracked the can open, then dropped down on the saggy bed. It gave an alarming creak.

All those dreams were gone.

It felt like a faded, distant dream.

It had all started when my mom had gotten sick. She'd battled cancer and I'd given up my dream of going to college in California to help dad take care of her. I'd attended a smaller, local college instead. We'd lost her just after my brother Elliot enrolled in the military.

I squeezed my eyes closed, as pain and grief swamped me. My fingers clenched the soda can. I missed my mom. The vibrant woman who'd loved to bake and hum as she did chores. Grief filled me like an endless sea. It ebbed and flowed, and every now and then, a wave came from nowhere and crashed over me, dragging me under.

I sipped the drink and tasted nothing.

I'd thrown myself into caring for my sister. Viv had grieved by going off the rails. I'd watched her get wilder and wilder. Our mother had named us. She'd wanted elegant names for her girls. Georgiana and Vivienne. She'd never once called us Georgie and Viv.

I rubbed between my eyes, willing my headache to go away, and sighed. "Oh, Viv." I'd tried to help her. Dad had been confused and had been no help at all. He was sure she was just going through a phase.

Then Elliot had died in Afghanistan.

Grief gripped me with sharp claws. That's when my family had split at the seams. The loss of him on top of my mother had been nearly debilitating. Dad died a year later of a broken heart. I'd finished college, but never gotten to live my dreams.

Nope, I'd learned that life didn't grant me dreams. It just liked to kick me in the teeth.

I'd worked at the local bank to get by. Meanwhile, Viv had dreams of being a singer.

"I'm going to be a famous popstar, Georgie. You'll see. One day, we'll drive down Rodeo Drive in a limo, sipping pink champagne."

The memory felt like a rock lodged in my stomach.

What Viv had gotten instead was a nightmare.

She'd been prey to the worst sort of predator. And now she was gone, too.

The grief of losing my sister was sharp and new, edged with fangs, and wrapped in guilt.

Oh, Viv.

All I had left was pain.

I was so damn alone.

Hunching my shoulders, I pulled my knees up to my chest, but I didn't cry.

I hadn't cried since Elliot's funeral. I couldn't. Everything felt like it was trapped inside me.

And I detested feeling sorry for myself. It didn't help a damn thing.

I shifted and set the can of Diet Coke on the cheap, scratched bedside table that looked like it was staying upright by prayer alone. As I moved, I felt my healing bruises tug and my arm ache. I should have my sling on.

Closing my eyes, I laid back on the lumpy pillows and hard mattress. I let one sneaky thought take over. The little thing I gave myself when I needed to feel less alone.

The memory of the boy I'd crushed on.

My brother's best friend.

Nathaniel Shawn Hagen.

Most people had called him Nathaniel or Nate, but those closest to him had called him Nash—an amalgam of the first few letters of his first and middle names. He'd lived down the street from us. His parents had been older, and he'd been a surprise baby for them later in life. He'd been tall, handsome, with thick, brown hair, and piercing blue eyes.

Smiling, I felt my frozen muscles loosen. I'd had so many teenage-girl fantasies about him. Of course, he hadn't seen me that way. I'd just been his best friend's pesky little sister.

Until he and Elliott had come back on leave from the Navy for my mom's funeral. I'd been seventeen, and he was twenty-one.

He was the most gorgeous creature I'd ever seen.

And finally, he'd seen me.

He'd given me the best kiss of my life under the maple tree in my parents' front yard.

I remembered that I'd trembled everywhere.

"So damn pretty, Georgie." He'd cupped my face. *"Grow up a little bit more. Use that clever brain of yours."* His thumb stroked over my cheek, and my eyelashes had fluttered, matching the butterflies in my belly. *"I'll be back."*

"Okay, Nash."

His blue eyes had bored into mine. "See you when I come back. Okay?"

It had been a promise.

I nodded. "I'll be waiting."

But when his parents died, he didn't come home.

It hadn't been a promise. It had been a lie.

Elliot hadn't said much except that Nash had been recruited into a special program, with special missions, and he couldn't get away.

When Elliot died, he hadn't come home.

When my dad died, he didn't come home, either.

I knew then that Nathaniel Hagen was never coming back.

Then Viv had needed me, and after being angry and sad at Nash, I'd locked his memory away.

But I did remember a rushed phone call with Elliot just before he'd died. It had been over a bad connection. He'd sounded tired and distracted, but he'd told me that if I was ever in trouble, to contact Nash.

He'll always help you out, Georgie. What he's turning into...he's enough to scare the biggest bad away.

Maybe Elliot had some subconscious inkling of his impending death in a firefight.

That had been the last time I'd spoken with my brother. Grief closed my throat. He'd died a hero in an ambush, saving several soldiers.

Then Viv had moved to Las Vegas to chase her dreams.

She'd taken one suitcase, her old, beaten-up car, three hundred dollars, and a head full of dreams.

Then, the life I'd once had was completely over. No family, no crush, no dream job.

I rose and went into the tiny bathroom to splash some water on my face. I ignored the mirror. I didn't need to see my healing black eye. The doctor had said I was lucky I hadn't lost any vision.

Back in the room, I grabbed a bag of chips I'd bought earlier and ripped it open. I had to get some calories into me.

My cellphone pinged and vibrated on the table.

Every muscle in my body went taut. I fought not to throw up the Diet Coke I'd drunk.

Woodenly, I reached for the phone. I had no friends anymore. I'd sold our house in Elk Falls. It was a funny thing when all your family died; a lot of your friends drifted away. I'd run into people on the street and they were awkward, didn't know what to say. I realized that my grief was a drag on their lives.

These days, only one person messaged me.

It didn't matter that I repeatedly changed my number. He still found me.

Steeling myself, I pressed my lips together and thumbed the screen. I'd learned that you had to face the shit life threw at you head on. Ignoring it, avoiding it, or trying to dodge it, none of that worked.

Nothing made it better anyway.

I clicked on the message.

The text was just an image.

Of my now-dead sister.

Bile filled my mouth. In it, she was kneeling and strung out, no doubt high on blow, with her mascara smudged. A naked man stood beside her, only his thigh and hard cock visible, her fingers wrapped around him.

I pressed delete.

Not that it would help. It wouldn't erase the image from my head, and the man who'd killed her would keep sending the images and videos.

He loved to torment me.

He was a sick fuck—rich, powerful, and untouchable. My hands curled into fists, my knuckles white.

He'd lured Viv with promises of a singing contract, and a gig in his hot Las Vegas club. He'd romanced her with flowers and dinners and expensive gifts. He'd gotten her addicted to cocaine, then started sharing her around with his friends, employees, business associates. He'd beaten her, abused her, and trafficked her.

Helplessness welled, but so did my rage.

Rage was so much better than sadness, grief, or help-lessness.

I grabbed onto it.

I'd come here to Las Vegas to save Viv. Instead, I'd gotten the shit beaten out of me, and now Viv was dead.

Now, I only had one thing to live for.

Taking down Dean Snyder.

Revenge, justice, retribution. I didn't care what it was called.

I wanted him to pay for Viv, and I wouldn't let him hurt another young woman with stars in her eyes.

He'd crushed what was left of my soul.

Now, he'd feel my rage.

Methodically, I grabbed the chips and made myself eat them, crunching on autopilot.

The memory of Nash, his low laugh that I'd loved, popped into my head, but I pushed it away. I'd thought about finding him. I'd actually contacted a hacker who'd said he could find anyone. He hadn't been able to find him. I took it as a sign that Nash was the past.

I was alone. There was nothing and no one to help me, but also no one to hold me back.

I would get revenge for my sister.

Whatever it took.

CHAPTER 3
NASH

I clipped some dead leaves off the plant. It was a gorgeous purple orchid. I leaned over it, checking the glossy, green leaves and air roots. In a few minutes I needed to head over to the Avernus security office to teach a training course.

The small greenhouse was filled with greenery and pops of vibrant color—red, pink, purple, yellow, white. It was just behind my villa.

When I'd first retired, Bastian had pestered me to find a hobby. He'd told me sleeping all day and drinking too much bourbon wasn't a good option. I'd been in the military for years. I'd been an assassin.

I had no idea what to do.

Bastian had been busy building the casino, and I'd pitched in with security, but I'd still been edgy, tense. I'd nearly gotten into several fights, and I'd known how easily I could kill some drunken jackass just for annoying me.

When I'd moved into the villa, Bastian had given me a housewarming gift of a potted orchid as a joke. The asshole expected me to kill it in under a week.

But I'd…enjoyed taking care of it. I'd ended up buying a bunch of different colors and types.

And much to my surprise, I was good at growing them.

I guess I shouldn't have been surprised, since my father had been a farmer and my mom had loved flowers. It had just been hard to believe that I could go from killing to actually growing living things.

Eventually, I'd built the greenhouse and the rest was history. I grabbed my watering can and carefully watered several plants. The air was humid and heavy. The Las Vegas climate was too dry for most of these plants, so that's why I'd needed the greenhouse. I'd learned about selective breeding and came up with my own hybrids. I had people who paid me a fortune for some of them.

It was worth it, even if the guys liked to give me shit about it, occasionally.

Sometimes, I came in here and just sat in the greenhouse in the quiet.

I turned and jolted.

A man was standing silently against the backdrop of my ferns.

"Fuck." I shook my head. "Make some damn noise and say hello like a normal person."

"Hello." His voice was deep, with a raspy edge.

"Asshole." I grabbed a cloth off the bench and wiped my hands. "I thought you were away."

"I'm back."

Alessio Rossi was officially retired. He'd once been the bogeyman of the Italian Mafia in New York. The former mafia enforcer and assassin had killed his way out of the life. That said, he still liked doing some unsanctioned side jobs.

He wore tailored suit pants and a white shirt. The shirt

contrasted with his bronze skin and the tattoos on his hands. I knew there was more ink under the cotton. He had dark, fathomless, brown eyes, and he was an intense, scary bastard. He'd given up the mafia life, but he lived by his own code.

One thing I knew about Alessio. He was loyal. To the bone.

He snuck off to do side jobs where he took out the worst of the worst. He especially hated those who preyed on women and children.

"I'm headed over to the casino to teach a close combat and takedown course with the security team." I paused. "Want to help?"

Alessio nodded.

He didn't talk much, but I didn't mind. We got on well, regardless.

I cleaned up and we took the path that snaked through the golf course to the shiny curve of bronze metal and glass that made up the Avernus casino's main building. The sun was out but it was cold today. December in Las Vegas usually brought cooler temperatures and some cloudy days. I bet back in Elk Falls there'd be snow on the ground. Sometimes I missed the snow.

Other villas neatly dotted the surrounding area. My gaze slid over Landon's, Cole's and Rafe's. Alessio's was tucked away out of sight. Bastian had a huge penthouse at the top of the casino.

"Job went okay?"

Alessio nodded. "Over quickly." He glanced sideways. "Are you okay?"

"Yeah."

"Bastian said there was a problem in the high-rollers suite last night."

I shrugged. "Three assholes decided to try and rob the high rollers. They brought in 3D-printed guns. We dealt with them."

"Bastian said you seem to be…off."

I rolled my eyes. "Damn, that man is like a mother hen. He pokes and pokes. I'm *fine*."

Alessio stayed silent. We reached the staff entrance, and I pressed my hand to the scanner. Alessio did the same. The lock beeped and the door opened.

The air inside the casino was cool and it washed over me. I could feel Alessio's gaze on me and I felt a sudden itch on my neck.

"I'm fine," I repeated.

Alessio just raised a dark brow.

"Hell." We stepped into the elevator and I stabbed a button. We zoomed down to the underground levels of the casino. The doors opened and I set off down the hall. "I thought you had to yank out teeth and fingernails to make people talk. Why do I feel like spilling my guts when you're just standing there saying nothing?"

Alessio made a sound. "I never yanked teeth. That's too messy."

"I am…okay. I work, I grow my flowers. I play poker with you assholes. What more do you want?"

"You're merely surviving, Nash. We want more than that for you. I get that we're all…private. We had jobs where we worked alone, but not anymore." He spread his hands. "For better or worse, we found each other."

"A fucked-up found family of killers."

Alessio's lips quirked. "Yes, but it works for us. It's our family. And no family is perfect."

I snorted. "Look, Bastian fucks and works, Landon is a workaholic at the clinic, you sneak off for side jobs, Cole participates in the underground fights. Rafe gallivants around the world collecting art and who knows what else. None of us are the poster child for well-adjusted."

"You're ours, whether you like it or not."

I blew out a breath. "I'm tired, and I don't fucking know why." I rubbed the back of my neck. "Now I'm late for the class."

Alessio kept pace beside me. "If you want to talk. I'm here. I also have an excellent bottle of Mitcher's."

I glanced at him. "How old?"

"Twenty-five years."

I whistled. I knew exactly how much that bottle of bourbon was worth.

Alessio shrugged. "It was a gift. For a job."

I pulled in a breath. "Thanks."

Moments later, we walked into the security office. The place was huge and Bastian had spared no expense. The computer and surveillance systems were top of the line. Right now, several of the security team sat monitoring the screens. They showed every angle of the casino. The system had advanced recognition and would alert them to any problems well before the human eye detected them.

When Bastian had first told me he was retiring and building a casino in Las Vegas, I'd thought he was crazy. He'd been one of the world's best-known assassins. Las Vegas seemed like a bad place to hide. But the first thing he'd done was have subtle facial surgery to alter some key facial components, like the bridge of the nose and cheek contours. Enough to throw off facial recognition. He'd also had his fingerprints removed.

Combined with creating an entirely new identity, it had meant he could hide in plain sight as Sebastian "Bastian" Thorne.

I'd had the same surgery. We all had. We still looked like ourselves, but we didn't register on facial rec as our old selves and we left no traceable fingerprints.

Alessio and I passed through to the large gym that was for the security staff's private use. Bastian had decked it out with the best machines and weights, a boxing ring, a large area covered in mats for training, and a shooting range.

There was a small group waiting for us.

"All right everyone, I'm Nash." The trainees all straightened. "My helper today is Alessio." I jerked my head at my friend. "We're going to teach you to quickly neutralize a threat here in the casino. Containing them as fast as possible is the priority, to limit the chance of anyone else getting hurt."

"What if they're bigger and stronger?" one man asked.

"It doesn't matter," I replied.

The young man frowned, his brows drawing together. "What?"

"You're going to learn the skills that you need to take anyone down. You're going to train and learn to execute with confidence."

The man didn't look convinced.

"What's your name?"

"Tyler."

I gestured for him to step forward. We were the same height and pretty evenly matched.

"I'm going to—" I gave him no warning. I attacked and executed a throw. He hit the mats on his back with an *oof* and I pinned him down with a knee to his chest.

The guy grunted.

I straightened, then held a hand out to help him up.

"You took me by surprise," Tyler said. "And we're the same height and weight."

"True. You have a few pounds on Alessio."

The young man glanced at my friend, and I could see that he thought he could take Alessio.

Tyler took one step toward the ex-mafia enforcer.

Alessio put him down in under three seconds.

Tyler landed on his knees, arm twisted up behind his back, chest heaving. Alessio looked bored.

The rest of the group whispered and nodded to each other. When Alessio released him, Tyler rose and stretched his shoulders.

"You're going to teach us that?"

I nodded. "We are. Okay, pair up."

Maybe peace in my life was elusive, but I had friends. I had this. I didn't need anything else.

CHAPTER 4
GEORGIE

I crouched on the roof and lifted the binoculars. Zooming in, I focused on the front door of Red Neon.

Bright neon lights blinked above the club door, along with a set of singing lips that was the club's logo.

My hands shook, my throat was so tight that I could barely swallow. There was a long line of clubgoers hungry to get in despite the cold wind. So many young women, dressed in their short, sparkly best, huddled inside their coats. Dressed up the same as Viv liked to do.

Ignoring the crowd, I swiveled and focused in on the two bouncers in black. I'd seen them around. The blond was Sam Alden, and the darker one was Mark Zanotti. They were part of Snyder's posse.

I'd also seen them in videos, using my sister.

My hands clenched on the binoculars. I kept a notebook. I printed out pictures of everyone and took notes on all of them.

Then the door of the club opened and a man stepped out.

My stomach dropped, a hot wave of rage washing over me.

He was about six feet tall and bulky. The one word to describe him was wide. He had a square jaw, pronounced brow, and a shaved head.

His name was Frank Bruno.

He was Snyder's right-hand man.

He was also the man who'd taken great delight in beating me up and putting me in the hospital. He'd almost broken my arm, bruised my ribs, and given me a black eye.

Bruno was a man I'd seen violently fucking my sister from behind while she cried and screamed. Nausea filled my throat and I almost vomited, but I fought for control.

I watched as he spoke to the other two bouncers, all of them laughing together. Bruno clapped Alden on the shoulder, his attention shifting to eye two barely legal women in short skirts at the front of the line. He lifted a meaty hand and waved for them to enter the club.

I couldn't hear from my vantage point, but I saw the young women squeal and follow Bruno inside.

Dragging in some deep breaths, I wrangled my emotions under control. I had to get inside. I wanted to see Snyder without him seeing me. I needed to know everything about his routine, the layout of his club, things he did on repeat.

Then I could find the best spot and time to take him down.

But seeing Bruno… I wanted to take him down, too.

He deserved it. They all deserved it.

I lifted my cellphone, thumbed the screen, and played a saved voice message from Viv. I'd replayed it so many times I knew the words by memory.

"Hey, Georgie." Her voice was a little shaky, but she wasn't high. I knew what that sounded like all too well. "I just...." A gusty sigh. "I just wanted to tell you that I love you. You're the best big sister a girl could have. The Linden Sisters against the world. See you soon."

I closed my eyes and played it again.

I'd never see her again.

I'd never see her smile, hear her sing, get one of her giant, enthusiastic hugs.

Snyder had trapped her, treated her like shit, abused his power.

He'd stolen something beautiful. My sister with the big laugh, the beautiful voice, and so much love in her heart, was dead.

Because of him.

I sucked in some deep breaths, the pain washing through me. Methodically, I put the binoculars back into my backpack. Swinging it onto my shoulder, I headed across the roof of the building across the street from Red Neon. I headed down the fire escape. My car was parked on a side street and when I reached it, I stuck the backpack in the trunk.

I checked my face in the reflection of the side mirror.

My blonde hair was tucked away under a black bob wig. I pulled out my lipstick and retouched my red lips. I'd gone heavy and dramatic with the makeup for two reasons. One, to look different, and two, to cover up the fading bruises around my eye. After I'd retouched my lips, I checked the dark contacts. I looked nothing like myself.

I straightened, smoothing a hand down my wide-legged black pants. I'd paired them with a tight red halter top that showed off plenty of cleavage. I'd lost weight recently but not off my breasts. I was also wearing a pair of killer red heels.

Shrugging out of my jacket, I tossed it into the trunk and ignored the cold that hit my bare arms.

Let's do this.

I headed for Red Neon.

If they recognize you, you'll be dead.

I lifted my chin. They wouldn't recognize me.

I bypassed the line, putting some swing into my hips and strode up to the bouncers. They turned my way, and I shot them a sultry smile, oozing confidence.

"Evening, gentlemen." I worked hard to block out all thoughts of what these men had done to my sister.

The bigger of the two, Alden, smiled, and jerked his head toward the door.

I blew him a kiss.

"Hey, we were next," someone in the line yelled.

I sauntered into the club and heard one of the bouncers say, "Damn, I want those red lips around my cock."

In your dreams, asshole.

It was dark inside the club, the music pumping and vibrating through my body. The walls were padded with black-and-red fabric, with touches of gold. As I stepped into the main room, lights strobed over the heaving mass of dancers grinding on the dance floor.

There were several circular bars dotted around the space and the bartenders were busy, keeping up with the thirsty crowd.

At the back of the club, the VIP areas were cordoned off with red ropes. There were more bouncers patrolling there. More men who'd hurt my sister. The VIP clubgoers sat on semi-circular, red-velvet couches, catered to by scantily dressed waitresses. The scraps of red and black silk barely rated being considered clothing.

I walked to the bar closest to the VIP area. I ordered a cocktail that I wouldn't drink and snagged a stool.

Sitting, I crossed my legs and pretended to sip. I made sure I didn't look like I was studying the VIP area. There was no sign of Snyder.

But he was here. Somewhere.

My gaze drifted to the door marked private. I knew it led to his office.

About now, he always came out. He had his own VIP couch, a little higher than the others. He usually invited women to join him for free drinks.

The music cut off and a voice came over the loud-speaker. "Hello! I hope you're all having a wild time tonight." The man had a smooth, deep voice made for radio.

The crowd screamed and cheered.

"You are very lucky. We have a special performance tonight. Only the best for Red Neonites."

More cheers.

"Say a huge welcome to our new feature singer, Shandy!"

I swiveled on the stool, ice filling my veins. I spotted Dean Snyder first, by the edge of the stage. He wore a white suit that glowed under the lights and a black tie. I hated that he was handsome—with styled, brown hair, a gym-fit body, and a perpetual half smirk on his lips.

He led a woman onto the stage, giving her a huge smile. Then he adjusted the microphone for her.

My heart shriveled. For a second, I thought it was Viv.

I blinked. The woman was taller and thinner than my sister, but had a similar mane of blonde hair.

"Evening, y'all." Shandy gave the crowd a shy smile. "I'm thrilled to be here and sing for you. It's a dream come true for me." She shot Snyder a pretty smile, then turned back to the crowd. "I'm gonna sing a favorite for you. I hope you enjoy."

The music started and I discovered Shandy had an excellent voice. I listened to her singing a song about hopes and dreams. Her voice was a little deeper and smokier than Viv's, but it brought back so many memories. Viv putting on performances at home from the time she could talk, using a hairbrush as her microphone. She'd sung at her high school graduation, and often did the national anthem at football games. She sang in the shower, she hummed as she read, she just lived and breathed music.

I miss you, Viv.

The music swelled, like it was responding to my grief, and Shandy hit her last note. As it faded away, the audience broke out in applause.

On stage, Shandy smiled. It was a little shy, but happy.

Then Snyder ascended the steps to the stage and held out a hand to her.

She took it with a wide smile.

I tried not to launch myself off the stool and attack him, but it was hard. My hand clenched on my glass. This was the man who'd systematically broken my sister.

Who'd killed her.

I watched Snyder lead Shandy to the VIP area. He was all charm, leaning in and touching her hair. No doubt complementing her performance, making promises he would never keep.

God, he was doing it again.

Dread flowed through me. Blindly, I lifted my drink

and took a long gulp. He'd replaced Viv, less than two weeks after murdering her, and now he was seducing this poor woman.

Soon, she'd be broken, raped, drug addicted.

Lost in my thoughts, I felt my cellphone vibrate, and it jolted me out of my despair. My gut cramped but I realized it couldn't be from Snyder. He was on the couch, canoodling with Shandy.

Blindly, I pulled my phone out and saw a message from an unknown number.

Your guy doesn't want to be found, and he keeps his shit tight, girly.

Oh God, it was from the hacker I'd paid a small fortune to find Nash. I'd given up on him weeks ago.

Got a single partial facial recognition. Might be him, might not be.

My chest squeezed. He'd found Nash. Maybe.

If I take more of your money, I'd be stealing from you.

Wow, I'd managed to find an upfront, honest hacker. I typed.

Where?

Avernus casino. Las Vegas.

My heart stopped. Nash was here? In Las Vegas?

Maybe. It might not be him. I tried to get control of my racing pulse. But surely this was some sort of sign.

I studied the image on the screen. It showed a man in jeans and a ball cap. The cap was navy blue, with no team logo or other markings on it. In the picture, he stood partly in profile, and it wasn't a clear view of his face. I zoomed in. He also had a beard. Nash didn't have a beard when I'd known him.

Was it Nash?

Maybe. I sure as hell didn't recognize the young man I'd crushed on in this hard, rough-looking man.

Even if I did find him, would he care? He'd left, he'd promised to come back, but he never had.

I was probably just a distant memory to him.

He was gone, like everyone else in my life.

He'll always help you out, Georgie. What he's turning into…he's enough to scare the biggest bad away.

He'll always help you out.

My brother's voice echoed in my head.

If Nash was as well-trained and as dangerous as Elliot had suggested…

Resolve tinged with electric excitement filled me.

I'd take one chance to see if I could find him, but I wasn't going to waste time on it. If I didn't find him, then screw it.

I stared at the photo on my phone again. Was the man spotted in the Avernus casino really Nash?

A part of me screamed that I didn't need him. That I was better off doing this myself.

The only person I could depend on was me.

Slipping off the stool, I headed for the door. I wasn't going to let Snyder use and kill another woman.

I was going to kill him.

But as I neared the door, I saw a group of Snyder's goons. Bruno and five others. They milled around, all relaxed and confident, sure they could get away with anything.

How the hell would I do this alone?

I had money. I could pay for help. My nose wrinkled. There was no one I trusted.

I headed for the exit, and my hand slipped into my pocket and clenched on my phone.

Having someone to help me might also increase my chances of actually killing Dean Snyder.

For that, I'd risk anything.

————

What the hell was I doing here?

Still in my outfit and black wig, I wandered through the casino floor at the Avernus.

The place was gorgeous.

It wasn't as tacky and in-your-face as some of the other casinos. It was like walking into classy sin.

The casino was done in black with bronze accents. The carpet was a plush black, with bronze geometric designs. Around me, poker machines sang and dinged. I wandered through, eyeing the cocktail waitresses and waiters. They looked just as classy as the rest of the place. They all wore black pants and shirts, topped with a bronze vest covered in an ornate pattern.

I passed a roulette wheel, clacking as it spun, my gaze skimming over the people laughing and playing.

They didn't seem to have a care in the world.

I'd already told myself I wasn't going to find Nash.

But a little voice sang to me that maybe it was fate.

It didn't matter. Whatever happened, if I had to take down Dean Snyder myself, I would. Hopefully in time to save Shandy, and any others he was grooming.

I caught the attention of a nearby server.

"What can I get you?" the woman asked, a friendly smile on her face.

"I'm looking for a friend." I pulled the folded piece of

paper out of my pocket. I'd stopped at a 24-hour printing place and printed out a copy of the photo. "I was told he comes here. Have you seen him?"

She glanced at the picture, her brow creasing. "He doesn't look familiar, honey. Sorry."

I nodded my thanks.

I checked the bar and got more head shakes. Dammit. This was turning into a wild-goose chase.

Spotting another server heading my way, I shot him my best smile. "Hi."

He smiled back, balancing a loaded tray of drinks like a pro. "Hi. You want to order something?"

"Not right now. I'm looking for my friend. Another friend said he'd been in here." I held up the picture.

The man's face stayed neutral, but I saw a flicker in his eyes. "Nope. Sorry. He looks like a hundred other guys who pass through here."

I stepped closer. "You know him."

The man's eyes widened. "I don't."

I grabbed his arm. "Please—"

He wrenched out of my hold. "I can't help you." He turned and hurried away.

Nash. Nash was here.

Or he had been.

"Sweet cheeks, I can be your friend."

I spun around. A guy wearing a baggy suit, in his late thirties or maybe early forties, was standing too close to me. He was holding a glass of whiskey, and he shot me a smile he probably thought was sexy. His face was flushed. This clearly wasn't his first glass.

"No, thanks." I turned.

An arm snaked around my middle. I stiffened, fighting the pain as he put pressure on my sore ribs.

"Let me go," I said through gritted teeth.

Hot breath brushed my ear and I smelled alcohol fumes.

"Sweetness, we can have *so* much fun together."

Anger speared up like a geyser. This guy thought he could ignore what I wanted, touch me without permission. I was fucking sick of assholes who thought they could just do whatever the hell they wanted to women.

I stomped my sharp heel down on the top of his foot. He cursed and bobbled his drink, spilling it over his hand. His arm loosened.

Spinning, I grabbed his other arm and twisted it up behind his back.

"Ow. *Ow*. Bitch."

"Oh, it's bitch now, not sweet cheeks?" I landed a hard shot to his ribs, and he sucked in a breath.

I twisted his arm some more.

He went up on his toes. "You're gonna break my arm!"

"Sounds like fun." I twisted a little more.

Out of the corner of my eye, I spotted security incoming, pushing through the crowd.

That was the last thing I needed.

I leaned in close. "Keep your hands to yourself next time." Releasing him, I strode into the crowd, letting myself disappear.

This was a waste of time.

I needed to be spending my energy on staking out Snyder and finding the right time to strike.

I'm doing this for you, Viv.

I ensured my pace stayed slow and steady. I walked unhurriedly out the front door of the casino. Even outside, I was careful to keep my pace measured, like I wasn't in a rush. *Nothing to see here.*

It wasn't until I was a block away, and getting close to where I parked my car, that I pulled the wig off. I shook my hair out.

I just wanted to get back to my hotel room, take my makeup off, and put my pajamas on. Maybe I'd find some action movie to watch and zone out.

I'd only taken a few more steps when I realized that I'd dropped the photo of Nash. I patted my pockets. No photo.

Oh well. It probably wasn't him.

Maybe it was a sign that it was time to forget about him, once and for all.

CHAPTER 5
NASH

UNSANCTIONED
SERIES

Bastian's office was huge.

I strode in, stretching my tight neck. I'd done several combat classes today. Shit, maybe I was getting too old for this.

The dark-wood floor was polished to a high gloss, Bastian's desk was a huge slab of black marble, shot through with bronze veins. A moody painting consisting of gray, black, and bronze smudges hung behind it.

"Evening." Bastian swiveled in his huge leather chair. The lights of Vegas shone behind him. Another man in a suit with his tie loosened stood at the front of the desk, knocking back a glass of bourbon.

Chance Tyler finished his drink and ran a hand through his blond hair.

"Long day?" I asked.

The actor lifted his chin. He was handsome in that clean, polished way that told me he had a great plastic surgeon and an excellent dentist. He looked like the kind of guy that would get cast as the district attorney or the president in a movie.

He no longer auditioned for movies. Instead, Bastian paid him a lot of money to pretend he was the owner of the Avernus. He did all the press, attended functions and events, and shmoozed when required.

"Had a group of high rollers in from China. They demanded I join them for poker, dinner, and a show."

I snorted. "Tough life."

"That was *yesterday*. I just managed to get free." He scraped a hand down his face. "I haven't slept in twenty-four hours."

"Go home, Chance," Bastian said.

The man waved a hand. "I will. I have a press conference and a council meeting in the morning. Its hard work being the fake owner of a casino." He headed for the door. "Night."

Bastian's gaze settled on me.

"You look like you need a drink, too," he said.

I jerked my chin. "Won't say no."

In an elegant move, he rose and stalked to the black cabinet against the side wall. He pulled out a bottle of something that was no doubt expensive and poured. I took the crystal glass from him and sipped. Probably Pappy Van Winkle. It should have tasted smooth, sweet, and spicy. Instead, it tasted like nothing.

I walked to the floor-to-ceiling windows. It felt like standing on the edge of a cliff, with a bird's eye view of everything. But tonight, it all blurred, my thoughts churning.

"The training went well?"

"Yeah." I swirled the bourbon. "Couple of the new team members are good. They have leadership potential."

"Excellent." I heard his chair wheel back. "Nash, we have a problem."

Turning, I raised an eyebrow. His tone was serious.

"What's up?"

"There was a woman on the casino floor tonight. She was looking for you."

Both my eyebrows winged up. "She asked for Nash Oakley?"

"No. She didn't use your name. She had this." He pulled a ratty, folded piece of paper from his pocket. He opened it and smoothed it on his desk.

It was an image of me walking in the casino. Thankfully, not a good picture.

"I thought with our alterations, facial rec wouldn't register against any old images of us."

Bastian shrugged a shoulder. "You're standing in profile. It probably used other factors. I mean, the image isn't great. It couldn't have been more than a partial match and whoever matched it must have used a hell of an algorithm, and a lot of time and effort."

Someone had come looking for me. My neck muscles tightened even more. "Who?"

"She said you're a friend, and she was looking for you."

Fuck. I felt a strange shiver. Whatever this was, I had a feeling it wasn't going to go away. I scowled. "Who is she?"

"I don't know." Bastian rose and circled the desk. He tapped on his sleek, silver laptop, then turned it to face my direction.

I saw instantly that it was security footage. It was frozen to show a perfect view of the woman standing in the casino.

I stepped closer and pulled the laptop across the desk. She was medium height, fit, slim body, with a killer set of breasts hugged by a red top. Her straight, black hair brushed her jaw, and her lips were a deep red.

I didn't know her.

My brow creased.

"No idea who she is?" Bastian asked.

"I've never seen her." My gaze ran along her jaw line, and I felt a whisper of…something.

"She could be an assassin. Hired by someone with an axe to grind. Maybe she's got her own axe to grind with you."

"We covered our tracks, Bastian." When we'd left our previous jobs, we'd taken steps. I'd been known as Nathaniel or Nate Hagen. Very few people knew I'd gone by Nash, and most of them were dead. "We have new identities. We did the work to kill off the men we'd been before."

"Maybe someone's cleverer than we thought."

I touched the screen and wondered who the hell she was.

Then Bastian reached past me and pressed a button on the keyboard. "Watch."

A guy in a bad suit grabbed the woman. My scowl deepened. *Asshole*. I had zero time for idiots who thought they could intimidate a woman.

Then a smile curled my lips. I watched her stomp on his foot, then twist his arm up behind his back and hand him his ass.

Suddenly I felt a rush of something else. For a second, I felt electric, awake. Energized.

Bastian made a sound. "I know that look."

"What look?" I scowled. "There's no look."

"You're impressed."

"Hard not to be." I cocked my head. "Despite some of the vapid women you bed, I know you like a spitfire."

My friend shot me an unreadable look. "This isn't about me."

No, Bastian liked to poke into other people's lives, but refused to discuss a certain female assassin who regularly tried to kill him.

"Where did she go?" I asked.

"She made a very cool, controlled escape before security arrived. She walked out the front doors, not in a rush, not attracting any attention."

"Facial rec get any hits?"

"Nothing. She hasn't been in the casino before, or any others in Las Vegas."

Who the hell was she?

And why was she looking for me?

Suddenly, I really wanted to find out.

"Send me the images."

Bastian nodded. "Done. I've got security watching for her. If she sets foot in here again, we'll know instantly."

I finished my drink. Now, I truly tasted it and enjoyed the spicy flavor. "I'll take care of her."

A smile curved Bastian's lips. "I'm sure you will."

———

"Rabbit, it's Nightvision." I kept the cellphone pressed to my ear as I walked into my villa.

"Nightvision. Long time, my friend."

I imagined him sitting in a dark room, with the glow of a screen in front of him. No doubt he'd be fidgeting and eating Doritos. He had a serious addiction, and constantly munched on them. Rabbit rarely left his condo.

He lived on one of the upper floors of the Sky Las Vegas tower.

We'd worked together a few times in the past. If you needed something or someone found, Rabbit was the one who could do it.

"I'm sending you an image of a woman." I tapped on my phone and emailed the image to an anonymous email address. I knew that it would get forwarded through various untraceable accounts, and finally uploaded to a private cloud server where Rabbit—the world's best hacker—would grab it.

"Sooo, Nightvision is after a woman," he drawled.

"It's not like that. She's been looking for me."

"Ah, she might be out to kill you."

I heard tapping. Rabbit had been in Naval Intelligence, before he'd had a breakdown and faked his own death.

Now he used his skills to do whatever the hell he wanted. Sometimes he did weeks-long gaming binges, other times he tracked down terrorists or corrupt politicians. His favorite thing was stealing from scammers who stole life savings from hard-working people. Whatever took his fancy.

"Nothing popping." Crunching came across the line, and I imagined Rabbit stuffing a handful of Doritos in his mouth. "I don't have a name for you."

Damn. That meant it might take Rabbit a few days to get something.

"But," he continued, "I can tell you she's walking down South 1st Street, just off Fremont."

I straightened. "Right now?"

"Right now. That help?"

"Yeah, that helps. I'll transfer your funds tonight. Thanks, Rabbit."

CHAPTER 6
GEORGIE

UNSANCTIONED
SERIES

I t felt like ants were crawling under my skin.

I couldn't sit still, I couldn't relax. I lengthened my stride, dodging various individuals and groups meandering down the street. There were families, loved-up couples, friends out for a good time. I sidestepped a couple canoodling as they wandered slowly, then a bunch of teenagers with skateboards tucked under their arms.

Sitting in my hotel room had been torture. The walls felt like they'd been closing in; my chest was too tight; my legs moving restlessly. I'd had to get out and do something.

Red and green lights blinked overhead. Christmas decorations hung across the street.

Christmas. Viv had loved Christmas, just like our mom had. Some of my best memories were family Christmases, with Viv tearing wrapping paper off her gifts, Elliot teasing her, and Mom and Dad watching on with indulgent smiles.

This would be my first Christmas without them all.

A lump lodged in my throat. Hunching my shoulders, I kept my head down, but my gaze was up.

On my target.

I'd dressed in something nondescript—jeans, boots, and a black hoodie. I'd had to do something.

Doing nothing was killing me.

Snyder had messaged me again. He'd sent me a video of Viv.

My stomach turned over at what I'd seen done to her.

God. I felt antsy. Energy throbbed inside me, desperate for a target.

I wanted to hurt Snyder. Hell, I wanted to hurt anyone.

My gaze locked on Frank Bruno walking ahead of me.

He walked like he owned the place. A man used to getting or taking whatever he wanted. I'd gone back to watch Red Neon and seen him leave.

It had taken me about two seconds to decide to follow him.

I bent my neck from side to side, listening to the cracks, relieving some tension. Then I slid a hand into the front pocket of my hoodie and my fingers closed around my stun gun.

I'd also purchased a handgun. It was wrapped in a shirt in my suitcase back at my motel room.

Some part of me wasn't ready to use that yet.

I didn't really know what I planned to do tonight. I just knew that I needed to do *something*.

Bruno was heading home. I knew that he had a nice apartment a few blocks off Fremont Street.

Yeah, the asshole did well for himself.

He turned into a quiet side street, and I picked up speed to keep him in view. I'd followed him before, and I knew he often took a shortcut through a dark alley.

Energy swelled inside me. This man had beaten me. He pinned me down, kicked me, punched me, and took great pleasure in tormenting me with all the things he'd done to my sister.

That sea of rage inside me roiled.

I closed in on him. He turned into the alley. It was dark here. There were no streetlights, no shiny storefronts, and there was no one around.

I should be afraid. I knew he was strong. If he got a hold of me...

Anger overcame the fear.

I had no fear left.

Whatever happened to me, there was no one left to care or grieve.

I stepped up behind him and he sensed me. He started to turn.

Quickly, I rammed a hard jab into his kidneys.

He grunted, his fist swinging out. "What the fuck?"

He caught me in my sore ribs. Pain exploded through my torso, but I ignored it. *Too late, asshole.*

I jammed the stun gun into his side and pressed the button.

He made a low sound as his body shuddered.

God, that felt good. I watched his body stiffen, the grimace on his face.

Finally, I wasn't afraid. I wasn't going to be pushed around. This time, I had the upper hand.

I stunned him again. And again.

His big body went down. He made a thump as he hit the dirty pavement. I followed on one knee and stunned him again.

He groaned. I slid the stun gun away and pulled a syringe and vial from my pocket.

Ketamine. A large enough dose to take him down.

I quickly injected him. His dark gaze—clouded and pained—locked on me. I knew the instant he recognized me. He moved weakly.

"It's Ketamine," I said. "You won't be able to move your limbs, but you won't stop breathing."

His eyes flared. I saw the fear and I reveled in it.

"How's it feel? Being helpless?" I pulled my arm back, curled my fingers into a fist and punched his gut. "Knowing I can do whatever I want to you?"

Air rushed from his lips, but he couldn't move.

"It's no fun to be trapped as someone beats you, is it?" I punched him again. "To be at someone's mercy." I lowered my voice. "How's it feel knowing I could hurt you? Like you did to me." My voice was a lethal hiss. "Like you did to my sister."

I pulled a knife, sliding it from its small leather sheath. I saw panic in his gaze now.

"I wonder what I should do to you next? How I can make you hurt? Where I can hurt you?" I held up the blade. "What I could cut off."

He made a low, animalistic sound.

"You deserve to be castrated. You deserve it all. You and that sick fuck of a boss."

I ran the knife tip down his cheek and pressed hard enough so that blood welled.

Could I kill him?

Could I move the knife to his neck? Could I cross that line? My stomach did a sickening turn. I wanted to, but everything in my life had taught me that taking a life was wrong.

But he deserves it.

Anger surged. Part of it for myself, for having doubts.

For hesitating.

Viv deserved so much better.

"Well, it seems you have him where you want him," a deep masculine voice drawled from behind me.

I stiffened. I hadn't heard a single footstep.

"Now what?" the voice asked.

CHAPTER 7
NASH

UNSANCTIONED
SERIES

The woman jerked to her feet.

The top of her head probably reached my shoulder. She looked at me, knife in hand, but I knew she couldn't see me clearly in the darkness. A nearby security light on one building gave the only illumination, and it was highlighting her and her victim.

"Stay back," she warned.

I held up a hand. "I figured he deserved it."

"He did." Her voice had a smoky undertone.

I cocked my head. "Are you going to finish it?"

She hesitated. She clearly wasn't a trained killer, but I felt a faint whiff of desperation. I knew desperation could drive people to do things they ordinarily wouldn't.

Being an assassin meant being cool, controlled, even detached. It paid to keep emotion out of it.

I'd watched this woman stun and drug the guy on the ground. She was a ball of emotion, running on it.

"What was your plan? Get him down, incapacitate him, then…?"

She licked her lips. She had very nice lips—full, still stained red. Damn, it had been a long time since I'd noticed a woman's lips. And the way she faced me head on, I liked that too. She was afraid, but she wasn't letting it stop her.

"I...don't know. I want to kill him."

The venom in her voice made my muscles tighten. *What had the bastard done to her?*

"You have the knife."

Her fingers tightened. "I... *Dammit*." She looked at the dirty ground.

Suddenly, the guy moved, his fingers circling her ankle. She kicked at him.

With a frown, I started forward. At that moment, sirens sounded at the end of the alley. Red and blue lights flickered.

The woman's face went blank, then she shoved the knife in her hoodie pocket, whirled and ran in the opposite direction.

Fuck, I hadn't asked who she was, or why she was looking for me.

If I lost her now, I might never find her again.

I ran after her.

She turned the corner and glanced back. She saw me following and picked up speed.

I kept her in sight. I was a runner and ran several miles each week. I could keep this up all day.

After a few more turns, she broke out onto Fremont Street.

Shit. I watched her run past a large Christmas tree decorated for the holidays and into the Fremont Street Experience. It was late, but it was still packed with people.

The iconic canopy overhead swirled with multi-colored lights. It was showing a Christmas theme, dousing everything in vibrant red, green, and gold. I kept my gaze locked on her. Thankfully, I was tall, and I could easily keep her dark head in sight.

Pushing through the crowd, I gained on her. The lights overhead changed to blue, dotted with snowflakes. I needed to talk with her, but I didn't want her to get hurt.

She ran into some people and two people fell to the ground with loud cries. Their bags spilled open, wallets, glasses, and keys spilling everywhere.

My quarry almost tripped, but she righted herself at the last second.

"Sorry, sorry." She spun and kept running.

I dodged the fallen people. Ahead, she turned a corner and I followed her into another dirty Vegas alley.

This was the type of alley that no one wanted to spend time in. It reeked, a rotting stench coming from the nearby dumpster. I heard her frantic footsteps ahead and I easily saw her in the darkness. My night vision had always been exceptional, even as a kid. Part of the reason I'd gotten my codename.

"I'm not going to hurt you," I called out.

"That's what they all say."

There was so much hurt and bitterness in her voice. I felt an unfamiliar tug in my chest.

I wanted to know who the fuck had hurt her.

"I only say what I mean." I pushed for more speed, closing the distance between us. She glanced back, and pumped her arms wildly.

Damn, she was quick.

My blood was pumping hard and I felt more alive than

I had in years. I realized that she was slowing a little, and I could hear her harsh panting.

"I just want to talk. Stop running. I could go all night, you know."

She snorted. "Guys always say that, too."

I cracked a smile.

"Just leave me alone."

"Not until you answer my questions."

"No."

She took another corner.

Damn, there was another busy street ahead. I heard people singing and laughing, no doubt coming to and from the casinos and clubs. I couldn't risk losing her again.

I leaped.

I hit her, and wrapped my arms around her body. I turned midair.

She fought me, twisting and struggling.

I landed on my back, the air rushing out of me. She landed on top of me and cursed. Then she turned into a she-devil, jerking and fighting. She rammed an elbow into my gut.

I rolled and pinned her to the dirty pavement. Nearby, a streetlight illuminated us in a pool of silver light. I grabbed her arms and pinned them above her head.

She snarled.

That's when I realized her hair was askew.

My brow creased. Not her hair. She was wearing a wig.

Blonde hair peeked from under it.

With one hand, I yanked it off and blonde waves spilled everywhere. Now I was close, I saw that her eyes weren't brown like they were in the casino security photos earlier. She'd obviously been wearing contacts and had taken them out, because now her eyes were hazel—a beautiful blend of green and brown.

Everything in me froze—my muscles, my heart, the air in my lungs.

No. It couldn't be.

"Georgie?"

CHAPTER 8
GEORGIE

UNSANCTIONED
SERIES

I couldn't breathe.

Partly because the man on top of me was heavy as hell, and partly because he knew my name.

I stared into his face. That hard, rugged face.

And piercing blue eyes.

My lungs locked. "Nathaniel?" My voice was the faintest whisper. My gaze ran over him. "Nash?"

I'd found him.

He released me, and in a swift move, pulled me to my feet. I kept staring at him, a wild mix of emotions storming through me. My throat closed.

In this hardened, tough man I didn't see any sign of the boy I'd known growing up.

"It's you," I whispered. "It's really you."

He was staring back like he didn't know me. "It's me. I go by Nash all the time now. Nash Oakley."

He'd changed his name. I suddenly felt cold. I had no idea what to say.

A part of me never truly believed I'd find him.

He reached out and I flinched.

He hesitated, then gently touched my face. A fierce scowl overtook his features. "You have bruises around your eye."

My hand whipped up. Crap, my makeup must've smudged off. I took a step back.

His arm whipped out and he hauled me back. He jostled my ribs and I let out a low cry.

His brows drew together. Then before I knew what he had planned, he pushed the hem of my hoodie up.

"Hey." I tried to push his hands away.

He hissed in a breath.

I was well-aware that my ribs were still mottled with bruises. It wasn't pretty.

"Who did this?" His voice cracked like a whip.

I stiffened, the hairs on the back of my neck rising. His tone was dark and filled with things that made my throat go dry.

"Georgie—"

"It's a long story."

His face hardened. "Then we'll go somewhere and you can tell it to me."

"I—"

He bent his knees, shifted his arms, then lifted me off my feet. I found myself in his arms.

By reflex, I clutched at his broad shoulders and then he was striding down the alley.

"Nash…" I swallowed. "You never came home."

A muscle ticked in his jaw. "I had my reasons."

Which were stronger than the urge to come back. To come back to me.

A ball of hurt spun in my belly. It shouldn't. We'd been little more than kids. But it did hurt. Thankfully, I'd gotten used to being hurt. I shoved it down low. "Where are you taking me?"

"Somewhere safe."

Nowhere was safe. I'd learned that lesson.

The monsters didn't always hide in the dark. They lived in plain sight, and people applauded them for everything they did.

Soon we were out on the busy street. Some people glanced at us, but this was Las Vegas. No doubt they'd seen crazier stuff than a man carrying a woman.

I felt the flex of his hard muscles in his chest. He was so much bigger and harder than I remembered. What had happened to him over the last ten years?

There was no give in him at all.

I wasn't surprised when he turned into the entrance of the Avernus Casino. Cars were pulling up, uniformed valets rushing out to open the doors.

He nodded at the security guard by the bronze front doors, then strode inside.

"Do you work here?" I asked.

Nash gave a low grunt, which wasn't really an answer.

He crossed the black and bronze lobby. A classy, modern-looking, bronze Christmas tree sat in the center of the glossy black floor. He didn't go near the long check-in desk, and instead headed to an elevator at the back. It wasn't in the bank of the main ones for the guests. It was clearly designed for staff.

He juggled me to the side and pressed a hand to a high-tech looking pad. It made a low beep and the doors opened. As soon as we stepped inside, the elevator whizzed downward.

When the doors opened, he carried me down a dark hall, and then shouldered his way into a room. A bare room. The walls were dark gray, and the only things in the room were a table, a few chairs, and a shiny glass window. I assumed it was a one-way mirror.

He sat me gently on the chair, then pulled a cellphone from his pocket. He stabbed at the screen and put it to his ear. "Theo? I need a first aid kit and ice pack in interview one." He paused. "Yeah. Thanks."

"I'm fine." I shifted on the chair. "My injuries are over a week old."

"That guy hit you in your side. It must have hurt like hell."

I sighed. "Okay, my ribs are sore, but that won't kill me."

He knelt beside me and my pulse went crazy. Warmth exuded from him, along with a crisp, citrus cologne. He wore a black shirt and black leather jacket, but my gaze fixated on the triangle of bronze skin at his neck. I wanted to push my face against his strong neck and breathe him in.

Warmth trickled through my belly, heading lower. I blinked. I hadn't felt a lick of desire in months. Not since I'd seen the first picture of Viv that Snyder had sent me.

"Who beat you?" Nash asked.

I straightened. "It doesn't matter—"

"I want to know who did this to you," he enunciated clearly.

"Nash." I grasped around for a change of subject. "Why did you change your name?"

"I didn't want to be found."

I flinched. So people like me, his past, couldn't find him. I looked over his shoulder at the bare wall. I shouldn't feel so hurt by that.

"Who?" The word was sharp, gruff. "I want a name."

I swallowed. "I left him sedated in that alley."

"Fuck." Nash shot to his feet. "You should've told me. I could've dealt with him."

I twisted my hands together. I wanted that, but more than anything, *I* wanted to be the one to deal with Bruno.

"Georgie?" Nash waited until I looked at him. "Who is he?"

I closed my eyes. "One of the men who hurt my sister."

Nash's brow creased. "Vivienne?"

I opened my eyes and nodded.

"When I tried to help her, *he* was ordered to teach me a lesson. He works for the man who abused and killed my sister."

Nash sucked in a breath, but his face stayed as impassive as ever. "Viv's dead?"

"Yes." Hollowness spilled through me, growing like a disease. "Everyone I ever loved is dead."

CHAPTER 9
NASH

One of the security team delivered a heavy-duty first aid kit. I sat it on the table and opened it. Resting on top was an ice pack.

I turned, holding the pack in my hand.

Looking at her was like a fist to my chest.

Georgie. Georgie Linden was here in front of me.

Then other emotions swelled. She was too thin, her smooth skin was bruised, and she looked tired.

Everyone I ever loved is dead.

My hand clenched on the ice. She was supposed to be living her happy, good life. She wasn't supposed to be hurt and hunched in a chair looking beaten.

Still, my gaze drank her in like I was parched and she was pure, cool water. She wasn't a girl anymore, or a young woman on the verge of adulthood.

She was all woman.

Her blonde hair—still the same starlight color I remembered—spilled around her slim shoulders. Her face was paler than it should be, but the freckles were there dotting her nose.

And those pretty hazel eyes.

They were watching me now, warily. She had sharp cheekbones and full lips.

I imagined kissing those lips.

I stomped on my thoughts. *She's hurt, asshole.*

Lifting the ice pack, I motioned at her hoodie.

She huffed out a breath. "Like I said., the injuries are healing—"

"And you got hit again today. Trust me, it will help."

With a huff, she yanked the hoodie up.

I saw the bottom of a plain, black bra, and those ugly bruises mottling her ribs. My jaw clenched, but I noted the slim, almost delicate, torso, and more of that smooth skin.

I pressed the ice pack to her side, and she hissed. Next, I pulled out antiseptic wipes and knelt beside her. Carefully, I wiped at a small graze on her temple, and got a better look at the bruising, now that the makeup was wiped away.

Rage could be hot, but it could also be cold and cutting. It welled inside me, spreading like cracks in a frozen lake.

That fucker had beaten her. Systematically. She was tiny compared to him, but he clearly hadn't hesitated. Not if her bruises were still this bad over a week later.

How bad had it been the day she'd been beaten?

Who had taken care of her? Who had helped her when she was in pain?

"Did you get treatment after this first happened?"

She nodded. "I woke up in the hospital."

The cracks intensified. The guy was a dead man. He just didn't know it yet.

"What happened to Viv?" I asked quietly.

Georgie was silent for a moment, then swallowed. "She was all I had left. Mom died, then Elliot, then Dad."

Elliot. God, I still missed my friend. He'd been a good, decent guy. He'd always been up for an adventure or willing to lend a hand.

When he'd died, I'd thrown all my grief over his loss into my work. To becoming the best, most effective assassin I could be. A part of me wanted to honor his sacrifice.

My gaze stayed locked on Georgie's face, and I saw her gaze turn inward.

"Viv loved to sing. She was good, too, and she wanted to be a star." Her voice sounded hollow. "Then Dean Snyder happened."

The name was vaguely familiar.

Her gaze flicked my way. "He's a club owner here in Las Vegas."

Those eyes turned haunted. I wanted to reach for her, but I stopped myself.

She wasn't mine. I wasn't good for her. She'd suffered enough and didn't need more crap heaped on top of her.

"He sold her dreams. Told her that he'd make her a star. She started singing in his club, and he was luring her along with the promise of a record deal. He also installed her in his bed."

I stayed still. I knew this story. I knew plenty of entitled assholes who used their power and money to get what they wanted.

"He got her addicted to drugs. Forced her to do whatever he wanted sexually. He withheld the record deal he'd promised." Sadness filled her face and her shoulders sagged. "Then he started sharing her with men. His inner circle, clients, friends. He filmed it."

Fucking hell. I took her hand. Her fingers were ice cold. "I'm sorry, Georgie."

"I came here to rescue her. I managed to get her away from him. I spent several days with her hunched on the floor of a hotel bathroom while she went through withdrawal."

There was a blank look on Georgie's face now and it hurt because I knew it hid so much pain.

"She was finally starting to feel a bit better. I went out to get food. He texted her and said he had some of her things to give her." Georgie rubbed her forehead. "When I got back to the hotel, she was gone, and not long later, he texted me a picture of her high and naked with two men. I went to the club to rescue her…"

And that's when she'd been beaten. "What happened next?"

"I woke up in the hospital. A few hours later, Viv's body was dumped in an alley a block away from the Strip. She'd overdosed. No one cared that he'd done it to her. To the cops, she was just another junkie."

"I'm sorry, Georgie. I'm sorry you lost her."

"The pain never stops." There were no tears in her eyes, but so much anguish. "I've lost everything."

"What about your job? Your home?" My stomach clenched. "Do you have a man?"

"No. I don't have any of that. All I want is revenge." Now, something sparked in her eyes and she straightened. "Snyder is doing it again. Seducing a new singer. And I'm certain Viv wasn't the first and won't be the last. He and the thugs he keeps around him have to be stopped."

"How are you going to do that?"

"I'm going to kill them."

Something inside me twisted. "Killing isn't always easy, Georgie. You had a chance tonight, but you couldn't take it."

She lifted her chin at an angle that radiated stubbornness. "I just need to be better prepared. I need to train and plan. I *will* stop them." She paused. "Elliot once told me that you'd scare anyone." She licked her lips. "And that you would help me."

I shoved a hand through my hair. "That's why you tried to find me?"

She nodded. "I didn't think I would. The person I paid to look for you…they said you didn't want to be found. But for Viv, I thought I'd try."

"I'm not some fucking white knight."

She rose and slammed the ice pack on the table. "Good. I don't need one. I need a dark one."

I threw out an arm. "This road is one you don't want to take." I paced the room, trying to get a grip on my agitation. Georgie killing anyone wasn't something I wanted for her. "Leave Vegas, Georgie. Go home. Go and live your life."

You could help her. Help her get revenge.

Help pretty Georgiana Linden kill. *Fuck.*

I was darkness. I didn't want her coated in the muck as well.

I wanted to save her from this.

I spun to face her.

"No. I'm not leaving." She crossed her arms over her chest. "Will you help me?"

"I want you to go back to Elk Falls. You have no idea what you're asking."

"No."

"You're not strong enough for this and you haven't got what it takes."

Her lips trembled. "I'm not that young girl anymore,

Nash." She gave a harsh laugh. "That small-town girl is long gone. Life ground her to dust."

I shook my head. My fingers curled into my palms to stop from reaching for her.

"I'll take that as a no." Her mouth flattened. "I'm sorry I ever came looking for you. Don't let me interrupt your life."

She shouldered past me, then slammed the door behind her.

I set my hands on my hips, looking at the floor. My chest was tighter than it ever had been.

Fuck.

This was for the best. She'd realize she couldn't do this, that she needed to go back to her life.

I didn't want blood on her hands.

CHAPTER 10
GEORGIE

The elevator spilled me out onto the main casino floor.

My chest was tight, my eyes were burning. Like I wanted to cry, but I couldn't. I pressed my hand to my face. I hadn't cried in so long.

Not when my father died. Not when Nash never came. Not even when I'd lost Viv.

I charged through the casino, the bells and whistles of the slots echoing in my ears. I already felt over-sensitized from everything that had happened tonight. Everything seemed to close in on me.

I should never have tried to find Nathaniel…Nash. He wasn't Nathaniel anymore. That dangerous, cold man was not the young man I'd known. That I'd thought myself in love with.

You're not strong enough. You don't have what it takes.

Screw him. I'd dealt with everything that life had thrown at me. I wouldn't let it break me.

I picked up speed, running through the casino, and stumbled outside. I gulped in air.

Parked outside were two Ferraris and a Lamborghini. Laughing people moved past me—some in jeans, others dressed in suits and evening gowns. Everyone was welcome at the casino to have fun and lose their money.

They were all going about their lives, and they had no idea other people were suffering. I had no life to go back to. I couldn't leave, not only because I had nothing left to go back to, but because I knew Snyder and his thugs would hurt more women.

They had to be stopped.

Next time, I wouldn't hesitate.

I'd prove to Nash that I did have what it took.

I strode onto the sidewalk and set my shoulders back. I needed a plan. One where I took out Snyder and Bruno, and preferably, didn't get caught.

I knew their routines. I knew they left the club at around 3 AM most nights.

They often had dinner at Sparrow + Wolf, one of the most well-known restaurants in Las Vegas, then drove together to the club. They'd spend the bulk of the night there, then they'd leave to head back to Snyder's mansion at 3 AM.

I'd take them out then. When they were sated, tired, and buzzed.

Resolve filled me.

I would do this. Alone.

I didn't need Nash. I only needed myself.

———

I carefully loaded the gun.

I could do this.

For Viv.

Shoving the gun in my bag, I slid out of my car.

A cool breeze danced around me, and I pulled my jacket closer. I was surprised at how cold the nights could get here in the winter. Even at three o'clock in the morning, Vegas wasn't asleep. Lights blinked from all directions, and I could hear shouts, laughter, and the thump of music.

I didn't let myself think of Nash.

There is just you. You're the only person you can count on.

I pulled out my phone as I walked and listened to the message from Viv.

"Hey, Georgie. I just... I just wanted to tell you that I love you."

I listened to the end. "I hope you're sipping pink champagne, Viv," I murmured.

I didn't care what happened to me now. If I survived this, and took out Snyder and his vultures, I'd get in my car and drive. As far away as possible.

I thought of Viv's grave in the cemetery here.

I hadn't been there. I'd still been in hospital when they'd buried her. I hadn't been able to make myself go to see her gravestone.

It didn't matter. She wasn't there anymore. She was flying free.

I stiffened my spine. The closer I got to Red Neon, the louder the distant thump of music. There was no line outside at this time. I nestled into the shadows across the street and waited.

Sure enough, like clockwork, Snyder's car—an expensive BMW sedan—pulled up, idling at the curb.

I dragged in a deep breath. He'd walk out soon.

I pulled out the gun. It felt heavy. My fingers clutched it.

I'd always been taught that taking a life was wrong. To trust in the law. I'd also been taught that bad guys didn't get away with their crimes.

Unfortunately, I'd learned that little nugget wasn't true.

The doors opened. I saw a group of giggling, tipsy clubgoers stumble out. The women were all arm in arm, laughing.

So carefree.

They disappeared down the street, then a second later, the door opened again.

Bruno walked out.

My heart hit my ribs. He was glancing back over his shoulder. He wasn't smiling but didn't look any worse for wear after my little attack earlier. Except for the bandaged cut on his cheek. I felt a spurt of satisfaction.

Alden followed him out.

Then Snyder.

I felt the roughness of the brick behind me and the cool air hitting my flushed skin. He wore a slick suit, and was smiling.

The singer was tucked under his arm.

My heart beat like a clock.

"Come on, baby, we'll party together at my place," Snyder drawled.

Shandy looked hesitant. "It's late…"

Reaching up, he tucked some of her blonde hair behind her ear. Then he lowered his head and nibbled at her lips.

Rage oozed out of my pores. Viv was barely in her grave.

"Frank really likes you." He nodded at Bruno and the man moved forward. He stepped up close behind the woman, too close. He set his big hands on her hips.

"And I like to watch," Snyder added.

She jolted. "Dean…I like *you*."

"I like you too, baby. So much. You want to make me happy, right?"

I'd had enough.

I lifted the gun and stalked forward. My hand shook a bit. *Dammit*. I gritted my teeth and firmed my grip.

This ended tonight.

I aimed and fired.

A bullet clipped Bruno. With a shout, he spun.

I fired again and again. The singer screamed. Snyder dove to the ground, dragging her with him.

The other guard fired at me.

I kept striding forward, uncaring. I fired at Alden. He fired back and I felt a burn across my arm. Gasping, I kept pulling the trigger.

Alden jerked and staggered back, hitting the front wall of the club.

I circled the car.

The woman looked up at me, tears and terror on her face.

"Do you see what he's really like, now? He's a monster. He wants to share you with his friends, record you, ruin you. Run." I waved the gun. "Run!"

She hesitated, then scrambled up and ran.

I turned the gun on Snyder. His face was twisted with rage, but I saw a flicker of fear.

"Just you and me, Snyder," I gritted out.

Then his gaze moved past me.

There was a flicker of movement, and that was the only warning I got.

Beefy arms wrapped around me and lifted me off my feet.

No! I'd forgotten about the last of Snyder's posse. Zanotti.

I fought. I kicked and jerked. The gun fell from my hands and hit the sidewalk.

"Big mistake, Georgiana." Snyder rose, dusting himself off. He nodded at Bruno

Bruno stepped in front of me. He raised his bulky arm, and the vicious backhand caught me in the face.

It hurt. Pain exploded through my skull and my eyes watered. I tasted blood.

"She's ballsy tonight. Attacking me. Drugging me." His next punch was to my sore ribs. I cried out. The pain made nausea rise inside me. "Shooting at us." He reached out and grabbed the bullet wound on my arm and jabbed a finger into it.

I bit my lip to hold back my scream. These assholes wouldn't get my screams.

"I warned you the first time not to come here," Bruno growled. "But you didn't learn."

Snyder stepped closer, smirking. "Now, we're going to teach you a very painful lesson about messing with me." He gripped my chin and forced my head up. "You might not survive this one."

CHAPTER 11
NASH

"Fuck."

I couldn't sleep. I pushed the sheet off my naked body. Slicing out of bed, I yanked on some jeans and a long-sleeved henley, and shoved my feet into my shoes.

I felt...tense and jittery. I'd fallen asleep for a bit, but it'd been fitful and restless.

I'd dreamed of Georgie.

Her pretty face, her bruises, her pain-filled eyes.

Everyone I love is dead.

My hands curled into fists, my muscles straining. I tried hard not to think of the look on her face as she'd left earlier. *Destroyed.*

My chin dropped to my chest. I couldn't believe that she'd lost everyone. She'd fought so hard to save her sister, and been hurt in the process, and still lost her.

She was alone.

If it wasn't for my fellow assassins, I'd be alone, too.

My jaw tightened and I ran a hand through my hair.

I'd made her leave. I didn't want to drag her into the darkness. She deserved the best, far better than a former assassin.

If she knew what I'd done for the best part of a decade, she'd run away as fast as she could.

She thought she wanted revenge, but once you crossed that line, once you took a life, there was no coming back.

I didn't want that for her. It was why I stayed away for years.

It's not your decision, asshole.

I walked through my dark villa. Things—nameless, uncomfortable things—churned inside me.

She'd leave Las Vegas. She'd go back to Elk Falls. She'd move on and heal.

With a growl, I opened the door and followed the path to my greenhouse.

It was dark as I stepped inside. The rich aroma of the plants and the sweet scent of blooms washed over me. It made me think of her. She'd always smelled sweet, like a springtime meadow.

But the woman tonight, she hadn't been sweet. She'd had a core of toughness inside and been running on grief and fumes.

I let my hand drift over the glossy leaves of an orchid, trying to clear my head. Trying to get Georgie out of it.

I'd spent years imagining her happy, healthy, smiling.

Yet, that wasn't reality. She was stuck in pain and darkness. She'd been hurt, was too thin, wasn't sleeping.

She deserved so much more. She deserved someone to take care of her and be her shield.

With a growl, I kicked the workbench, setting empty pots shaking. Dragging in a breath, I tried to find some calm.

Being calm right now was fucking impossible.

I didn't stop to think. Whirling, I strode out and headed toward the casino.

Now, I was worried about her. If she went after Snyder and his men again...

She had no one.

No, that wasn't true. She had me.

I had all the skills needed to help her, protect her, keep her safe.

I needed to find her.

It only took me a few minutes to get to the security room. As I shouldered through the door, I barely paid any attention to the wall of the screens and the men and women manning them.

One of the team looked up from the screens. "Hey, Nash. Late for you to be here."

I lifted my chin. "I have some things I need to check, Michelle." My gaze flicked to the busy screens. "Everything okay?"

She gave me a faint smile. "It's been a quiet night so far. We've only had one card counter, a couple of college kids trying to use tech to cheat, four drunken fights, one handbag snatcher, and one flasher. The night's still got a bit of time to throw us a challenge."

I nodded. "I'll be in the office, if you need me."

I opened the door to the small office I sometimes used. I dropped down in the seat behind the desk and touched the mouse to wake the computer. After entering my password, I quickly tapped on the keyboard to access the casino's facial recognition system.

All the casinos used them. It helped weed out the cheats, the criminals, and the troublemakers.

I inputted Georgie's photo. The one of her from my

wallet. It was true her face had changed as she'd matured into a woman, but the key characteristics were the same.

I rubbed my thumb over the photo. That carefree smile was long gone.

Who the fuck was Dean Snyder?

I thought of the man hurting her, abusing Viv, and it left me enraged. While the facial recognition worked, I looked up Snyder.

He looked like a smarmy bastard. Handsome, entitled. There were lots of pictures of him at Vegas parties and events, and several with Viv by his side. She looked a little like Georgie, but her hair was curlier and her body curvier.

Fuck. At first, Viv looked pretty and vibrant, dressed up in short, glittering dresses. But the later photos showed her thinner, strung out, her eyes haunted.

Nothing overt popped about Snyder. His nightclub looked legal. At least, at first glance. The guy had a little power and money, and I suspected he used it to manipulate women.

Okay, now I felt compelled to deal with him.

The computer beeped.

There were no hits on Georgie in any of the casinos.

I hesitated for a second, then tapped again. I'd made a few modifications to the system. It meant that we could tap into all the public CCTV in Las Vegas.

It wasn't legal, but I didn't give a fuck.

Barely a second later, I got a hit.

I leaned forward. It was video feed from a street. I frowned. It was outside Snyder's club, Red Neon.

My insides froze. Georgie. With a gun in her hand.

She was striding across the street to a group of men. I recognized Snyder.

She fired, and men scattered.

What she didn't see was the asshole sneaking up on her.

When the man grabbed her, my body locked.

When another big guy rose from a crouch and slapped her face, I was on my feet and running.

CHAPTER 12
GEORGIE

I'd stopped struggling.

I didn't just feel pain, I was pain. A throbbing ball of it.

We were still outside Red Neon. Some people had tried to leave the club, but as soon as they'd opened the door and seen what was happening, they'd quickly gone back inside.

No one was coming to help me.

I tasted blood. One of my eyes was swollen shut.

Bruno was still hitting me, the other guard holding me immobile.

Snyder stood by watching, smiling.

I hated him so much.

Why? Why did such bad people get away with such terrible things?

Life wasn't fair.

Bruno landed another blow to my stomach. I moaned, nausea washing over me. I wouldn't last much longer.

They'd kill me. They'd dump me in an alley like trash, just like they had done with Viv.

No one would miss me. No one would mourn me.

I had nothing and no one who cared.

That hurt worse than the blows.

Suddenly, I heard a sharp crack.

I blinked, confused. Maybe they'd broken a bone?

Then I was falling.

Snyder was shouting, his words unintelligible. I hit the pavement, but I was in too much agony to move. Then I realized the guard who'd been holding me, Zanotti, was on the ground, as well. I gingerly turned my head. He was lying still, and there was a hole between his dark eyes.

What?

My foggy brain tried to process it. Then I spotted Snyder scrambling away. Bruno was shielding him. There were more cracking sounds. Gunshots. They were slow. Careful. Controlled.

Bruno jerked, and red bloomed on his shirt. He waved his gun around, firing wildly and blindly.

The pair of them dove into the backseat of the car.

More bullets hit the metal. The car fishtailed as it sped away, its engine revving.

Then there was just the sound of my own ragged breathing and nothing but pain.

I heard the sound of running footsteps. I tensed. Was it another guard?

Then I saw Nash's face.

"Fuck, sweetheart." There was a brief touch on my face. "They're gone. I've got you."

I tried to talk, but my lips were bloody and I couldn't form the words. I managed a low gurgle.

"Shh. Easy." He eased his arms under me and lifted me.

Pain flared to life everywhere. A small cry escaped me.

"I know, sweetheart. I'm sorry, I know it hurts. I need to get you out of here."

I closed my eyes. Nash was carrying me. It felt like a dream.

Then I felt him stop. He was standing in the shadows and I heard his voice. It took me a second to realize he was talking on the phone.

"Landon, it's me. I need your help."

I drifted in and out of consciousness. I loved the low rumble of his voice. So deep, sexy.

"She's been beaten badly. Can you come and get us? We're on the corner of—"

I breathed in his scent. Dimly, I realized he must have come here on foot. It was a long way from the Avernus.

"Okay, thanks, man. See you soon. Hurry."

Gently, he shifted me in his arms.

"N-Nash."

"Yeah, Georgie. I'm here. I'm going to take care of you."

"You…came."

"Yes. I realized you were in trouble. I ran here as fast as I could."

I thought for a second that I heard a shake in his voice.

"Hell, if I was a little later…" He made a low sound. "I'm going to look after you and keep you safe." He paused. "You had the chance to walk away, but you didn't. Now, you'll have to deal with the consequences."

I wasn't sure what he was talking about.

I drifted in and out of consciousness, listening to his steady heartbeat under my ear. I felt warm in his arms. And not alone. The pain didn't seem quite as bad.

I had no idea how much time had passed, but the rumble of a car engine brought me back.

"Finally," Nash muttered.

A car door slammed. "Fuck. What happened to her?" a low, masculine voice said.

"She's been beaten. She has a gunshot wound to the arm. It's a flesh wound, thankfully." He sounded so angry.

"You kill the fucker who did this?"

The other male voice was angry, too, but he had a really sexy voice, with a touch of a rasp.

"One of them," Nash replied. "The others ran, but I'll catch them."

There was a dark promise in his voice. A lethal one. I shivered.

"Easy, Georgie." His tone softened.

The next thing I knew, I was being carefully laid on the back seat of an SUV.

I couldn't stop a whimper. Everything hurt.

"I know, sweetheart." A hand brushed over my hair. "Soon. You got any painkillers?"

"I brought my kit. I'll give her something. She have any allergies?"

Nash leaned over me. "Sweetheart, you have any allergies?"

"No…"

Then I felt a small prick in my arm.

"Nash, is this…?" The man made a sound. "She's the picture in your wallet."

"Yes." Nash sounded like he was talking through gritted teeth.

"Hell, okay. Clinic?"

"No, my place."

There was a long pause. "All right, but if I think she has any broken bones or internal bleeding, she'll need the clinic."

"Fine, but she's staying with me. Where I can take care of her. Where I can protect her."

His words didn't make any sense. No one took care of me. I looked after everyone else, and failed in all of that. They all died.

That was my last thought before the pain faded away, then so did everything else.

CHAPTER 13
NASH

Very carefully, I carried Georgie into my villa.

I ignored my barely used guest room and entered my own bedroom. I laid her gently on the king bed. She looked so feminine compared to the bold, masculine colors of my room.

She stirred.

"Shh." I stroked her hair.

She settled again and I flicked on the bedside lamp. Damn, her face. My chest constricted. It was so battered. There'd be more bruises tomorrow, and now her lip was split and her eye swollen. I was afraid I'd hurt her if I touched her.

"Her name's Georgie?" Landon sat beside her on the bed. He opened his black medical bag.

He'd left his assassin career long behind, then whizzed through medical school in record time. Now, he put everything into helping others his own way.

"Georgiana Linden. Prettiest girl in Elk Falls, Idaho. My best friend's sister."

"Ah." He started examining her. "Forbidden fruit."

If Elliot could see her now, he'd lose his mind, then go on a rampage to punish those who'd hurt her.

I've got her, buddy.

Landon checked her pulse, then shone a light in her eyes. It always amazed me that those big hands—hands that had killed so many times—could be so gentle. I'd seen him give kids lollipops to stop their tears and make them giggle. I'd watched him calm the most frightened patient.

"Get some ice for her face, Nash. We need to get the swelling on that eye down."

I nodded. I hated leaving her. After getting some ice packs from my freezer, I was back as fast as I could. I sat on the other side of the bed and pressed an ice pack to the side of her face.

She whimpered.

I gritted my teeth. I hated that she was in pain.

She was done being hurt. I wouldn't let anything touch her ever again.

"Her pain hurts you."

I glanced at Landon. He was watching me, curiosity on his face.

"Yes. I tried to stay away from her. After I entered the program…"

Landon and I were both products of the same CIA program. I'd been trained to be a lone, deadly shooter. He'd been trained with the blade, to take his targets out up close and personal.

I knew of all of us, Landon was probably the most dangerous.

"When I got out, I didn't go home, I didn't look her up." God, how many times a day had I wanted to pick up the phone, to go home, to find her. "I didn't want to…contaminate her."

Understanding darkened his eyes.

"She was supposed to be living golden. Having every-thing she wanted, everything she deserved…"

Fuck, I wanted to punch something, or someone.

"We both know life doesn't work like that. Sometimes the bad guys prosper, the good guys suffer."

I touched her hair. "I won't let that continue, not for her."

My friend shot me a faint smile. "Good. We have the skills to balance the odds a little." He reached for the hem of her hoodie and pushed it up.

I tensed. Landon was my friend, but I didn't like seeing his hands on her. Anyone's hands on her.

A growl I couldn't control escaped my lips.

Landon cocked a brow. "Easy. I'm a doctor, remember."

I watched as he palpated her stomach.

"I don't detect any broken ribs, and no signs of internal bleeding, but we'll have to keep an eye on her. Put an ice pack here too."

I added another one to her stomach. She made a sound, and I smoothed my hand over her hair again, soothing her.

Landon checked the bullet wound on her upper arm. The bullet had left a nasty crease in her bicep. I ground my teeth together. He cleaned and bandaged it.

"I'll leave some painkillers. She needs rest. I'll check on her tomorrow. Clean up the blood and get her in some clean clothes."

"I've got it."

"She's underweight."

"She won't be for long." I rubbed the strands of her hair through my fingers. "Thanks, Landon."

With a nod, he collected his bag. "Call me if she needs anything." Then he was gone.

Carefully, I stripped Georgie out of her bloody clothes. I had to cut the hoodie off so I didn't hurt her.

I uncovered a long, slim body that was too thin. She'd been running on stress, anger, and grief for too long.

We'd fix that. I gently unhooked her bra and pulled it off, leaving her panties on.

Hell. I tried not to look at her pretty, pink nipples. Despite the fact that she'd clearly lost weight, she still had full breasts. They were the perfect size.

You're an asshole, Oakley.

I detoured to the bathroom and returned with a bowl of warm water and a cloth. I gently washed the blood off her skin.

"I promise, no one will ever hurt you again." I rinsed the cloth in the bowl and squeezed. I wiped the blood away from her arm. "Whatever you need, I'll get it for you. You're done suffering, Georgie. If life wants to throw shit at you, I'll stand in front of you and deflect it."

The feelings I'd held back for years surged up. It was like a lock had been broken and a door flung open.

"I'll protect you. I'll kill for you. Whatever you need. If *anyone* tries to hurt you, I'll burn the world down for you." I stroked a strand of hair off her face. "Snyder, Bruno, and the others are going to pay." Even in sleep, she turned her head, pressing her cheek into my palm.

My cellphone vibrated in my pocket. I'd turned off the ringtone so that it didn't disturb her.

Pulling it out, I saw Bastian's name on the screen.

I put it to my ear and rose from the bed. "Hey."

"I've got Landon in my office. He said you've got your dream girl there."

"Georgie. Her name's Georgie." I pulled in a breath,

walking to the doorway so I didn't disturb her. "Bastian, I need your help."

"Anything, you know that. Landon's mad as hell. Said she's hurt badly. A bunch of guys way bigger than her beat her up." There was disgust in Bastian's voice.

"I need to find out everything you can find on a man called Dean Snyder, and the men he keeps around him. He owns a nightclub."

"Shit."

"You know him?"

"Yeah. He's an asshole."

I looked down at Georgie. "I'm well aware of that."

"I don't know him well, but I'm on it. I'll find out whatever I can, along with whatever secrets he's keeping. Whatever you and your girl need."

My girl.

"Thanks, Bastian."

"Take care of her. We'll talk later."

I slipped the phone away, and on the bed, Georgie moved restlessly. I sat beside her and brushed my fingers across her uninjured cheekbone.

"Shh, I'm here, Georgie. You're not alone."

She settled against my pillow instantly.

And I sat there in the darkness and watched her breathe. I stayed there until the pale light of dawn peeked around the curtains.

CHAPTER 14
GEORGIE

G od, how had my lumpy motel bed turned so soft and comfy?

Hmm, I must be having a good dream.

I opened my eyes. Sunlight filled the room in the way only bright Las Vegas sunshine could.

I froze.

This was *not* my crappy motel room. I blinked rapidly.

The room was decorated in dark grays and blues. A sleek, wooden dresser was pressed against the wall. A framed photo of Las Vegas at night hung above it.

I turned my head and noted three things. One, there was a vase of gorgeous orchids on the bedside table. They were white and purple, and so beautiful.

Two, I was hurt. I felt a familiar tightness in my face and my ribs were aching again. I lifted my hand and gently probed the swelling around my eye. Yep, it wasn't good, but I wasn't in agony. I had vague recollections of someone urging me to take some pills. A deep voice cloaked in darkness.

Three, the sheets smelled like Nash.

Nash.

Oh God.

I shot into a sitting position, which jolted me and sent several shots of pain through me. I swallowed a moan and touched my ribs. Bruno hadn't gone easy.

Hell. The entire 3 AM attack hit me in gory detail. I'd blundered in and almost gotten myself killed.

Nash had saved me.

I was in Nash's bed. And it looked like I was wearing his T-shirt. I plucked at the soft cotton that looked like it had been washed many, many times.

The bedroom door opened and the man in question strode in.

Suddenly, my aches faded. He wore a pair of jeans that looked ancient and hugged his strong thighs. I suspected they hugged his ass, as well, but I couldn't confirm from this angle.

I didn't have time to contemplate that, because he wasn't wearing a shirt. His chest was fully on display.

Oh. The jolt of desire I felt was at odds with getting beaten nearly to a pulp. Yet, all that tan skin, all those muscles…

The man had abs that made me itch to touch. I twisted my hands together in my lap. He had a light dusting of brown hair across his pecs. A man's chest. Not some pretty, waxed and oiled calendar model.

"Hey." He was carrying a wooden tray. "How are you feeling?"

"Um… Okay."

He set the tray down beside the flowers on the bedside table.

Where had ex-military badass Nash gotten orchids?

"I made you some breakfast." The bed depressed as he sat down.

He was so close to me. All that glorious chest was so close. I swallowed.

"How's the pain level?" he asked.

Pain? Oh, right. "Okay."

His gaze narrowed. "You telling me the truth?"

I nodded.

"Good. You can't have more painkillers for a little bit. But now, you need to eat."

"Nash." I grabbed his wrist and his blue eyes met mine. Then his gaze wandered to my eye, and I saw his face harden. I winced. "It looks bad, doesn't it? It'll be even worse tomorrow."

A muscle ticked in his jaw. "Snyder and his guys are dead men."

I shivered. "Thank you. For saving me."

He cupped the uninjured side of my face. "I won't let anyone ever hurt you again."

My heart felt like it swelled to twice its size. I wanted to believe him, but life had shown me time and again that I was one of its favorite punching bags.

Nash handed me a glass of orange juice. "Drink." Then he leaned over and shoved some pillows behind my back.

My nose was an inch from his pec. I felt a rush of heat between my legs. I sucked in air and breathed him in.

"Here we go." He flicked out the legs of the tray and settled it over my lap.

I looked at all the food and blinked. There were pancakes—a tower of them—a bowl of sliced fruit, toast, scrambled eggs, and bacon.

"You made this?" I asked bemused, sipping the juice and setting the glass on the tray.

His lips twitched. "I want to say yes, but I ordered it from room service."

"Room service?" I looked around again. "But this is your house."

He nodded. "It is. I live in a villa at the Avernus Casino."

"Oh, wow."

"Living in a casino has some benefits. Now eat up."

"Nash, there is *no* way I can eat all of this."

"You're too thin. You haven't been taking care of yourself."

"I've been a little busy." I thought of Viv and sadness welled in my chest.

Nash leaned over and cut off a piece of pancake, then held the fork to my mouth. Obediently, I ate. The sweet taste of maple syrup exploded across my tongue.

"I had your car brought here. Do you have a hotel room somewhere?"

"Such as it is. At the Park Pines."

He gave a quick nod. "I'll send someone to check you out and grab your things."

"What?" I shot him a confused look.

He lifted another forkful of pancake to my mouth. "You're staying here. With me. You're going to get better, and I'll take care of you."

I hurriedly swallowed my mouthful of food. My lips parted and I felt a burning prickle in my eyes. How long had it been since someone had taken care of me?

Not since Elliot had been alive.

"Nash—"

"No arguing, Georgie. Not today. Snyder is still a risk to you, and I need to keep you safe. And you need to rest, eat, and heal."

There was no way I could fight him on this. I couldn't even get out of bed.

So I ate until I was stuffed. He helped himself to some of the bacon that I couldn't eat, grabbed the tray, and set it on the nightstand.

"I really can't impose on you."

His face got a mutinous look. "You're not going anywhere."

"Nash, I can't—"

Suddenly, he whipped the sheet back, and before I could worry about everything being covered, he lifted me out of the bed.

"What are you doing?" I asked breathlessly.

"Showing you something you might like."

You naked? God. Heat hit my cheeks. "I think you're just trying to distract me so I can't argue with you."

He carried me through the living room and shot me a crooked smile. "No idea what you're talking about."

The living room definitely said 'single man lives here'. There was a large, black leather couch, large TV, and a distinct lack of knickknacks or collectibles. I did note lots of books on the bookshelf against the far wall.

By the front door, he set me down, then nabbed a brown suede jacket off a hook. He wrapped it around me.

"It's sunny today, but still cold. Don't want you getting a chill."

He opened the front door and scooped me up again. I squinted at the bright sunlight. He was right, the air was cool and swirled around my bare legs. He strode down a path, but didn't go far. I saw our destination was a small greenhouse.

Oh. The glass walls were filled with green. He managed to hold me and open the door.

Inside was lush and humid, and I was assaulted by different scents. The rich scents of earth, of green things growing, and fertilizer.

"What is this place?"

"My greenhouse."

"Yours?" I looked up at his rugged face. "You grew all of this?"

Suddenly, he looked uncomfortable. "Yeah. Seemed like a good hobby."

I wriggled and he set me down. He held my elbows until I was sure I had my balance. Clutching the jacket with one hand so it didn't slide off, I studied a yellow orchid beside me and reached out to touch it. "It's incredible, Nash."

He relaxed. "Ah...thanks. I was pretty surprised to find I was good at growing things."

There were lots of different plants and flowers, at differing stages, but most of the flowers were orchids.

"I make some of my own hybrids."

My attention flew to a gorgeous, pretty, white one. "Really?"

"People buy them from me." He almost sounded surprised.

"Wow. I think this one is my favorite." I pointed to a smaller orchid. It was white, with a pink center, tiny purple dots across it, and a frilly edge.

"Mine too." His voice was thick. "It's one of mine. One of the first ones I created."

I glanced over my shoulder. "What's it called?"

He paused for a second and I thought I saw a blush in his cheeks underneath the stubble.

"Georgiana. It's called Georgiana."

My heart stopped.

He'd created a flower and named it after me. Had he thought of me all these years?

He hadn't forgotten me?

"Come on, you should sit down." He led me to a bench nestled in the greenery. "I want you to rest."

For just a little while, I wanted to hide from reality. To stay here in the lush greenery, just the two of us.

Where I had no dead parents, no dead brother and sister.

And there was no Dean Snyder.

I sank onto the bench and breathed deeply.

But I knew I couldn't run away from reality. No matter how much I wished I could.

"Nash, about Snyder—"

Nash sat beside me and held up a hand. "Not today."

"But—"

He shook his head. "Today, you let me take care of you and nothing else. Okay?"

I bit my lip, then nodded.

"Good. Now, I'm going to fill the watering can and I'll let you water the flowers."

CHAPTER 15
NASH

UNSANCTIONED
SERIES

My arms crossed over my chest, I watched Bastian, Cole, Landon, and Alessio stalk into my villa like they owned the place.

Well, technically Bastian did, I guess.

"How is she?" Landon asked.

"Sore. She's napping." It was late afternoon now, and I'd bullied Georgie into eating again and taking some meds. We'd watched some TV, but she'd been tired and had started falling asleep.

I'd tucked her into my bed and then I'd watched her sleep for a while, spending time counting the freckles sprinkled over her nose. I got the impression she hadn't had a good sleep for a long time.

That would be changing.

"I'll check on her before I leave." Landon set his medical bag down, then sat on a stool at my kitchen island. Cole leaned against the counter. Bastian sat on the couch, while Alessio stood. The guy wasn't good at relaxing or switching off.

"I've got the security team digging into Snyder,"

Bastian said. "He owns the Red Neon nightclub. That's his main business. He does a few record deals and has a DJ business with a fleet of DJs that he hires out for events."

"All aboveboard?" I asked.

"Mostly. He deals with some shady people. I wouldn't be surprised if he's laundering money for some clients. He's never been charged with anything, but he certainly does business with people known to bend the rules. He also owns a lot of real estate, including a big mansion in Summerlin."

I frowned. I'd been hoping for more.

"He also has a pattern of abusing women," Bastian added, voice sharp.

I tensed, and the others did, too.

Alessio's gaze sharpened, burning black.

"Like he did to Georgie's sister Viv," I said.

Bastian nodded, distaste on his face. "The fucker uses the same play every time. He likes to play the big man. Lures them into his club, puts them in the spotlight, promises them a record deal. Then he throws cash around, spoils them, seduces them, puts them on a pedestal."

"Love bombing," Landon said.

"What?" I frowned.

"It's over-the-top lavishing of attention, gifts, and flattery on someone. To manipulate and influence them."

Bastian leaned forward. "That's exactly it. Once he has them hooked and isolated from their friends and family, he shows his real colors."

"Georgie said he started sharing Viv with his men, clients." My lip curled. "He also videoed it." *The sick fuck.*

Bastian nodded. "Looks like he also gets them hooked on drugs. He's all about control."

"Classic abusive asshole," Landon said.

"He has money, and power and control over their careers," I added. "Viv ODed. She was found dead in an alley. Georgie says Snyder killed her."

"It's likely," Bastian said. "But you'll never prove it. He'll have evidence that she was a drug addict. No doubt he'll earnestly show that he tried to help her."

I let out a growl. "His right-hand guy beat the shit out of Georgie. Twice."

Bastian made a sound. "Frank Bruno. Ex-boxer and a nasty piece of work."

"I've seen him around the underground fights," Cole said. "He likes to use his fists."

A hot ball lodged in my chest. "Georgie tried to save her sister. Last night, she tried to kill Snyder and Bruno. One of the other guards jumped her and Bruno beat her again."

"She's lucky she's alive," Landon said.

My gut cramped. If I hadn't woken up…

If I hadn't checked on her…

She could've died, and I wouldn't have known. I tasted bile. I reminded myself that she was safe in my bed.

"You killed one of Snyder's men," Bastian said. "Mark Zanotti. Nice shot, by the way. Single T-zone shot between the eyes. He had a long record of assault and rape charges against several ex-girlfriends. We scrubbed all the CCTV. There's no record of you or Georgie being there. My source at LVMPD said Snyder claimed it was just a random shooting."

I grunted. He wouldn't want the police looking too closely. "I had Theo bring her stuff over. She was staying at this seedy motel off the Strip." Theo had told me he wouldn't let his dog sleep there, and he'd seen two drug deals going down in the parking lot while he'd been there.

Bastian leaned back against my couch, but I could tell he wasn't relaxed. Not one little bit. "Your Georgie's sister isn't the only one."

My head jerked. "Come again?"

"I looked back a few years. Five of his singers that he was fucking are dead."

"Five," I whispered.

Bastian nodded, rage in his eyes. "Three ODs, one drowned in the bathtub, and another hanged herself."

"Jesus," Landon said.

Alessio said nothing, just prowled the edge of my living room. A muscle in Cole's jaw ticked.

"And the cops ignored it?" I asked.

"They haven't linked him to it." Bastian spread his hands. "They just see ODs and suicides."

"Bullshit." The word was like a bullet. "Fine." I sliced a hand through the air. "If the law won't stop him, I will."

"You want to go unsanctioned?" Bastian lifted a brow.

"Hell, yeah. I'll stop him."

"*We* will," Landon said. "You're not in this alone. Georgie is yours, and you're ours."

I looked at them all. "I want Bruno, as well."

Bastian nodded.

"No," a female voice said. "They're *mine* to kill."

I jerked around. Georgie stood in the doorway, leaning against the doorframe. She was only wearing one of my T-shirts, which thankfully swamped her and came to mid-thigh.

I closed the distance between us. "You shouldn't be out of bed." Something in me twisted. I didn't want anyone seeing those bare legs but me.

She took a step forward, wobbled. I grabbed her arm, and thankfully she leaned on me. The bruises around her eye were darker, lots of black and purple. I locked my rage down.

She looked at the others. Her gaze moved to Landon.

"I know you." Her brow creased, like she was fighting to remember.

"Landon," he said.

"He treated you last night," I said.

"I remember your voice. Thank you."

"Georgie, this is Landon Bradshaw. Bastian Thorne is the one on the couch."

Bastian inclined his head.

"Alessio Rossi." I nodded my head. "And Cole Black."

Alessio dipped his chin and Cole nodded.

"These are your friends?" she asked.

"Most of the time."

Bastian snorted.

"Snyder is *my* problem." Georgie lifted her chin. "He killed my sister. He's evil."

I saw my friends look at her, felt their anger at her injuries.

"I'll take care of it," I told her.

"No." There was a spark in her eyes. "I want to. I *want* revenge. I want to take him down."

I felt rage vibrating from inside her.

"I'll help you," Landon said.

She blinked. "But you're a doctor."

He shot her a faint smile. "Most of the time."

I touched her shoulder, fingers curling around the delicate joint. "Before, years ago, we were all...something different."

She blinked. "What were you? You were all in the military?"

"Not exactly." I drew in a breath. "We're all good at killing."

An unreadable look crossed her face. "I don't understand."

"We were all trained to take out our targets."

Now understanding moved through her eyes. She glanced at the others before focusing back on my face. "Assassins?" she whispered.

I stayed silent.

"This is why you didn't come home?"

I stiffened, waiting for her to back away, to gasp, to look at me in horror.

But there was no horror on her face. Her gaze stayed locked on mine, then she pressed her palm to my chest.

"Nash…"

"I'll help, too," Alessio said.

Georgie blinked. "You don't even know me."

"I'm in, as well," Cole added.

Bastian shrugged a shoulder. "I'm not missing out on the fun."

Dammit. Big hazel eyes locked on my face. I cupped her cheek. "We'll help you."

CHAPTER 16
GEORGIE

UNSANCTIONED
SERIES

T he next morning, I felt well enough for a shower.

I'd slept like a rock for fourteen hours. After I'd met Nash's attractive but scary friends, Landon had checked me over.

I'd fallen asleep while eating dinner. Nash had ordered me to bed and tucked me in again.

I shivered. I'd slept my first dreamless sleep that I'd had in weeks, maybe months. The painkillers probably helped.

Stepping into his bathroom, I glanced around. He'd brought all my things from the motel, so now I had makeup and clean clothes. My nose wrinkled. Although a part of me was sad to give up his soft T-shirt.

The bathroom was nice. It was done in a matching, masculine vibe to the bedroom. There was a mix of dark-gray tiles and lighter concrete. The large, glassed-in shower had a huge rain-shower head.

Then I turned and saw myself in the circular mirror above the sink.

Oh God. My stomach dropped. I didn't look so nice.

I looked like an extra from a horror movie. One side of my face was covered in multiple bruises that were currently a shade I'd call putrid grape. I lifted the shirt and saw the blotchy bruising covering my torso.

Wow. I looked…terrible. There was no way I could hide the bruises. I sucked in a breath. This was only temporary. I'd heal.

And Snyder and Bruno would pay.

I turned the shower on. Nash and his friends said they'd help me take down Snyder and his posse. I pressed my hands to my chest, a flush of hope filling me.

Nash hadn't confirmed that they were assassins, but I knew it in my gut. They'd been trained to take down bad guys. As much as this felt like my problem to deal with, there was no way I'd turn away from that help.

The renewed hope spread. I had a purpose.

"I'm doing this for you, Viv," I murmured.

I wouldn't let her death be in vain.

I stepped under the water, which stung when it hit my bruises. I winced and adjusted the spray. I was moving slower than I would've liked, but I reminded myself that it could have been much worse. It took me forever to wash my hair, but being clean felt good. The shampoo smelled citrusy like Nate. A tingling sensation filled my belly.

After shutting off the water, I stepped out. As I grabbed a towel, a wave of dizziness hit.

"Shit." I staggered, the towel in one hand, while I grabbed at the vanity with the other. I knocked over a can of deodorant, and it clattered to the floor.

"Georgie!" The door flew open and Nash barreled inside.

We both froze.

His eyes dropped to my breasts. I didn't cover my naked body.

His gaze burned into me and traveled down my body. There were more bruises, and I knew I'd lost weight over the last few months. Self-consciousness crept up like a giddy enemy.

But he didn't seem to care. Heat flared in his eyes.

"I'm okay." I shakily wrapped the towel around me.

He looked at me for another beat. "You sure?"

I nodded.

"Get dressed. After breakfast, we're starting."

"Starting what?"

"Your training."

"My training?" God, I sounded like a parrot.

His lips twitched. "Yes. We're starting with some time at the shooting range. Next time you shoot at Snyder, you'll hit him."

Nash turned and strode out.

My chest swelled. He was really going to help me.

He was going to help me kill Snyder.

I wasn't alone anymore.

The hot sting of tears threatened, but as always, they didn't fall. Which was fine with me. I had no time for tears. I had to focus on my mission.

I dried off my hair and pulled it back in a damp pony-tail. I did my best to cover my bruising. It was a losing battle, but as I stared at the dark marks, they served as a reminder that what I was doing was right.

From my suitcase, I dug out my favorite sage-green leggings, a black T-shirt, and a light zip-up jacket. I wriggled into the leggings. They were the most formfitting things I'd worn in ages.

For a second, I felt like myself again.

My gaze snagged on the bedside table and I sucked in a breath. There was a pretty orchid—this one potted—sitting there. The flowers were a bright, happy yellow.

My throat tightened. Flowers, food, someone looking out for me. *Don't get used to this, Georgie.*

"Bagel, cream cheese, and smoked salmon," Nash said, as I entered the living area. He pointed to the island. "Sit. Eat."

"You're bossier than I remember." I zipped up my jacket.

"If you want to do this, you need to be in top form."

I sat on the stool. "I want to do it." I met his gaze. "Does that make me a bad person?"

"What do you think?"

"I think Snyder is going to keep hurting people, unless someone does something." I studied Nash's rugged face. "I think it depends why someone kills. If you kill in self-defense, no one considers that a crime. If you kill because you like it and enjoy hurting people, then it's wrong. If you kill someone who's evil and hurts other people…I think that's forgivable."

His blue gaze held mine for a moment, then he nodded. "Coffee?"

I groaned. "Yes, please."

"Still take it with creamer and one sugar?"

I blinked, shocked that he'd remembered. "Yes."

We ate and I gratefully sipped my coffee. I realized that I was starving and devoured my bagel. "So where is this shooting range?"

"Here."

My eyebrows winged up. "At the casino?"

"Yes, although it's not open to the public. It's for the security team to use."

That was so cool. I watched him over the rim of my mug. "So you, Landon, and the others all served in the military together?"

He was quiet for a beat. "No."

I frowned. "Landon seems like he was military."

"He was. Army. The others weren't." His gaze locked on me. A long, probing look. "I was recruited into...a special program."

I felt goosebumps cover my arms. "What kind of program?" I wanted to know. I wanted to know everything about Nash.

He lifted his coffee and took a long sip. "When I said we'd all killed, it wasn't just on the battlefield."

I suddenly felt cold. "I know."

"We were sanctioned to kill the enemies of our country."

"So I was right. You were an assassin."

"I know what it means to take a life, Georgie. Deliberately. With thought."

I swallowed and set the mug down. I understood now what Elliot had meant. "Do you regret it?"

"No. The people I killed... We're better off with them gone."

I lifted my chin. "Good. That's how I feel about Snyder, Bruno, and the others. The cops will never be able to stop them. And Snyder will continue to hurt and kill people. *You're* what I need, Nash."

There was a flash in his eyes.

"The others...your friends, they're assassins as well?"

"We're all retired. We weren't all in the same program." He paused. "We weren't always sanctioned."

"Okay, well, you and your friends have the skills that I

need. I'm not here to judge." I pushed my empty plate away. "Now, how about we go to the shooting range?"

CHAPTER 17
NASH

UNSANCTIONED
SERIES

"**H**old it steady. Squeeze slowly and take your time."

I stood behind Georgie. She was holding a Glock handgun and wearing ear protection.

The range at the Avernus was underground, with dark concrete walls and several lanes. A tablet at each station controlled the targets.

Following my instructions, she fired.

It went wide. She was still anticipating the shots and jerking as she fired.

I wasn't really worried. We'd get her there. I nodded and she lowered the gun.

As I slipped my earmuffs down around my neck, she did the same. I pressed a button and the paper target whizzed toward us. She'd gotten in a few good shots, but quite a few were at the edge of the paper.

Her nose wrinkled. "I *definitely* need some more practice."

"You'll get better." I glanced at my watch. We'd been

here for a couple of hours, already. I could see she was rapidly beginning to tire.

Fuck, I hated those bruises on her face. There was still some swelling, but her split lip was already scabbing over.

"Let's head back to my place. We'll have a light lunch, you can rest a bit, then tonight, I'll let you pick the movie we watch."

Her lips curled. "What if I want to watch a romcom?"

"Then a romcom it is." I'd suffered through worse.

"Lucky for you, I like action movies." Her smile faded. "I can't help but feel I should be doing something about Snyder—"

I grabbed her hand. "Heal first. We'll train and get you ready. He isn't going anywhere."

She nibbled the unhurt part of her bottom lip and nodded. "I should do one more round."

"You've done enough for today."

She stepped closer to me and her breasts brushed against my chest. I felt like I'd been hit by electric shock. I was so aware of her.

"Nash?"

"Yeah." My voice was croaky.

She reached up and pressed a palm to my cheek. I felt that touch in so many places. Places that had been parched, dried, and cracked for so long.

"Thank you," she murmured. "For helping me. I know you didn't want to. That first night, you wanted me to leave."

I pressed my hand over hers. "It wasn't that. I just didn't want this life for you. Darkness, killing. It's not you."

"Life doesn't always give us what we expect. It's about facing our challenges, making the most of things."

My gaze fell to her lips. *Control, man.* Her injuries helped me dig deep and find it.

I cleared my throat. "One more round?"

She smiled and nodded. She slid her hearing protection back on, and I organized the next target.

She reloaded the handgun—she was getting good at that now after I'd drilled her on doing it when we'd first arrived.

She took the correct stance, her face focused.

I couldn't look away from her pretty face.

She fired.

After she was finished, she eagerly ditched the gun and earmuffs. "That felt better," she said excitedly. "I was more relaxed."

More of her shots on target. "Nice work."

She shot me a beaming smile. Then she did a little victory dance. Now I was staring at her ass as she wiggled it. Those leggings showed the shape of it perfectly.

She spun, her smile still wide. It was so reminiscent of the Georgie I remembered. She threw her arms around my neck.

I stilled. The world spun as her entire body pressed against all of mine.

Her smile faded and different emotions coalesced in her hazel eyes. "Nash," she murmured.

Then she went up on her toes and pressed her lips to mine.

My brain short-circuited. I couldn't move. I stood there like a frozen idiot.

She pulled back, heat hitting her cheeks. "God, sorry. I...really wanted to kiss you. I should've asked, not just assumed—"

I gripped her arms. "Georgie."

"Nash, I'm sorry—"

"Georgie, be quiet."

She stilled and licked her lips. "Okay."

"I want to kiss you, but I don't want to hurt you." My thumb brushed her healing lip.

Her chest rose and fell.

"And I don't want you to feel that you owe me anything."

She shook her head. "It's not that at all."

I slid a hand into her hair and her lips parted. God, those bruises made me mad. "You have bruises, a sore lip…"

"Can you be gentle, Nash?" she whispered.

My gut tightened. "I never have been before. But for you, I'll do anything."

"Then please kiss me."

I lowered my head and touched my mouth on hers.

I had to fight my instincts, my flaring desire. I gently kissed her, being careful with her lip. If she knew what I really wanted to do to her, she might not be so eager.

She moaned and opened her mouth. I explored. God, she tasted like sunshine.

So much poured through me. Memories of this girl had gotten me through some dark places.

It had always been her.

Her tongue stroked mine and I groaned.

We had to stop. Before I hurt her. That, I wouldn't allow.

I lifted my head. She blinked, her face dazed and flushed.

I wanted to spend a lot of time putting that look on her face. "Still the prettiest girl in Elk Falls."

She smiled. "I'm not a girl anymore."

No, she wasn't.

I tucked a strand of her starlight hair behind her ear. "Come on. Lunch time."

CHAPTER 18
GEORGIE

"**H**ere you go."

I took the candy bar that Nash shoved at me. "I'm not really hungry."

"Eat it. You need the energy."

Wrinkling my nose, I unwrapped the Snickers bar and took a bite. We'd just finished our second session at the shooting range. He'd woken me this morning with a huge breakfast again, then told me we were heading to the range.

He was all in with taking care of me. I felt flutters in my belly. He was feeding me constantly, checking if I needed pain meds, always gauging if I was tired. Last night, as promised, he'd let me select the movie. We'd watched the latest Mission Impossible adventure while we snuggled on his big, leather couch, my feet in his lap.

When I'd fallen asleep, he'd carried me to the bedroom, and given me a sweet, gentle goodnight kiss.

Yes, my tough, muscled former assassin could be very gentle.

He was sleeping in the guest room, but every fiber of my being wanted him in the same bed as me.

Guilt trickled in. Viv was dead and here I was thinking about sleeping with Nash.

I swallowed, my throat dry. Besides, I couldn't let myself get too attached. He'd walked away from me once before. I knew how much it hurt to lose those you loved.

Love was too much of a risk.

The elevator doors opened and Nash pressed a hand to my lower back. When we stepped outside, he didn't take the path toward his villa.

"I thought I'd show you a little of the casino grounds," he said.

I was pretty sure that was code for getting me to have some exercise with a short walk. I munched on the rest of my candy bar and followed him down another path.

A huge, circular pool came into view.

It was too cold for swimming, but the pool looked immaculate. It was flanked by wooden pool loungers and dark-wood cabanas. They all had carved metal sides and breezy white curtains. I bet it was amazing in the warm weather.

"It is truly an honor for the Avernus to support such a worthy cause," a smooth, masculine voice said.

We circled a large garden bed and ahead, I saw a man in a glossy suit standing at a microphone. He was blindly handsome, with a square jaw, perfectly styled blond hair and very white teeth. He looked like he should be an evening newsreader or doing commercials. There was a group of people nearby, some clearly press who were holding cameras and taking notes. Beside the man was an oversize check resting on a stand.

Nash pulled me into the shade under a tree where no one would spot us.

"The Avernus couldn't think of a better charity to support than Veterans Village. Ensuring all our heroes have safe, affordable homes, and the resources they and their families need is vital. Thank you."

Flashes blinked as the man shook hands with a woman and handed over the check.

"Mr. Tyler? Chance?" a reporter called out. "The Avernus has a history of helping veterans. What's next for your casino in regards to your favorite cause?"

The man smiled. "I believe our Events team is planning a charity golf tournament and a spectacular gala ball. More details to come soon."

"That went well."

Bastian's voice made me jolt. I saw him standing on the other side of Nash. I hadn't heard or sensed him join us. He wore a suit that was tailored to his trim form. I realized that he was roughly the same height and weight as Nash, but the suits hid it well.

"Looks like it," Nash agreed.

"That man owns the Avernus?" I really thought he belonged in a commercial, for toothpaste or expensive cars.

Nash chuckled. "Chance? No, he doesn't, but everyone thinks he does."

My brow creased.

Nash jerked a thumb at Bastian. "He owns the place."

Bastian dusted off the shoulder of his jacket. "Considering my previous…employment, I had no desire to be the face of the casino. Chance does it for me and is well compensated."

Now my eyebrows winged up. "So you can run the place from the shadows?"

He smiled at me. "I'm quite fond of the shadows." He tilted his head. "Your face is looking better today."

"Thanks." He was being nice. The swelling had gone down, but my bruising was still impressive. At least my lip was almost healed.

"I'll leave you to it," Bastian said. "I have a meeting to get to. Let's do dinner soon." He winked at me. "Georgie, I look forward to getting to know you better."

Nash scowled. "Don't wink at her."

That just made Bastian laugh. I watched him stride away. The way he moved was mesmerizing.

Nash took my hand and we ended up back on the path to his villa. "We need to check the orchids."

"Can I water them again?"

"Yes."

"So, you grow orchids, Landon became a doctor, and Bastian owns a casino."

"Yes. He built the place."

"It must have cost a fortune."

"Bastian was CIA. On his last job, he…stumbled across something valuable his target was hiding. Anyway, he had his reasons for leaving the life, and decided to put the windfall to good use."

"What, like stumbled on a vault filled with gold?" I joked.

"No. Several bags of uncut diamonds."

My mouth dropped open.

"He built the Avernus with the sale of the diamonds. People fight to get a job here. He pays the highest wages and offers the best health insurance and benefits."

And supported charities for veterans. "Why Avernus? Where does the name come from?"

Nash's lips quirked. "It's the name of a volcanic crater and lake in Italy. It's said to be an entrance to the underworld in Roman mythology."

"And he's a former assassin, so the underworld fits."

"The best restaurant in the casino is Elysium."

I gasped. *Elysium.* I'd heard of the restaurant before. It had a top chef and a months' long waiting list for a table. "Elysium is like heaven in Greek mythology, right?"

"It was a part of the Greek underworld reserved for the good and heroic, or those chosen by the gods."

His greenhouse came into view and he tugged me closer.

"What about Cole and Alessio?" I asked. "What do they do?"

"You probably don't want to know."

"I can tell they weren't military."

"No, they were not." He opened the greenhouse door, and we stepped into the lush confines. "A story for another day."

I pulled in a deep breath of mixed scents—soil, fragrance, and fertilizer. Soon, I had a green watering can in hand, watering the orchids that needed it. Nash went to a workbench to work on some orchids he was propagating.

When I finished, I sat on a low, wooden bench nestled right in the center of the space. From here, you couldn't even tell you were in a city, let alone Las Vegas. I felt a sense of peace drift through me. I wondered how many times Nash had sat here.

My gaze shifted to him, where he was bent over his workbench. I'd dreamed about him so many times, and here he was—big, strong, and oh-so-real. Taking care of me, helping me, keeping me safe.

I knew I couldn't let myself get used to this, couldn't depend on him too much. But fighting the pull of him was impossible.

Rising, I set the can down and walked toward him.

His head lifted. "You getting tired? We can head back to the villa."

"I'm okay." I saw the orchid on the bench and I gasped. "Nash, that's incredible."

The blooms were blue. Several lush flowers were on the stem, with a delicate yellow center. I'd never seen anything like it.

"Blue orchids are rare," he said. "You can get some in the shops, but they're regular orchids that have dye injected into them."

I pulled a face.

"This one is an Australian orchid that is one of the few, naturally blue ones. The flowers bloom in the morning and close in the evening."

"It's gorgeous."

He wiped his hands on a rag and reached up. As he tucked a strand of my hair behind my ear, I suppressed a shiver.

Being with him, it was making so much come back to life inside me.

"Not as gorgeous as you."

His words speared through me and I met his gaze. "I need something."

"Anything. Whatever you need."

"I need you to kiss me."

He groaned. "Georgie…"

"My lip is almost healed."

"I couldn't stand it if I hurt you."

My hands clenched on his shirt, twisting in the fabric. "You'll hurt me if you don't kiss me. I need you to make me feel, show me this is real and not some dream that I'm going to wake up from and—"

His hand slid into my hair, tilting my face up.

My heart tripped, then raced. "Nash…"

His mouth closed over mine. He wasn't rough, and I knew he was still being careful. I felt the sensation of his beard against my cheeks, his tongue tangled with mine, and I moaned at the taste of him.

With a low sound, he kissed me deeper and hauled me closer. I was plastered against him, my hands gripping his firm arms. I felt the length of his cock, trapped behind denim, pressing into my stomach.

Yes. This. The feel of him, the taste of him, made me forget everything. I slid my hand under his shirt, finding the smooth, warm skin of his back. My fingers brushed over a lump, which had to be a nasty scar, but I didn't let that derail my exploration.

Then he broke the kiss and pressed his forehead to mine. We were both breathing heavily.

"That's enough for now." His voice was low, gritty.

I let out a sigh.

His fingers, and the calluses on them, brushed my jaw, making me look up.

"I thought the best kiss I'd ever had was under that tree in your parents' yard. This one was even better."

I swallowed. "You remembered that kiss?"

"Never forgot it. Thought about you a lot, when I was in some…not nice places." He stroked my cheekbone, then stepped back. "It must be time for you—"

"If you say to eat, I'm going to scream. You just fed me a candy bar. I'm going to pop from all the food."

He smiled and didn't look very sorry. "I'll make you a smoothie."

I sighed. "That's food, Nash."

"You'll like it, I promise."

CHAPTER 19
NASH

I gently sifted my hands through Georgie's hair.

She was asleep on the couch, her head in my lap. We'd decided to watch an old favorite tonight and put on Predator. It had been Elliot's favorite movie. Somewhere between watching Arnie cover himself in mud and build booby traps to take down the alien predator, she'd conked out.

Her bruises were slowly getting better. They weren't quite as dark and there was some yellow now. I stroked her hair, marveling at the pale color.

I was enjoying taking care of her, but I knew as she got stronger, she'd want to know when we could take down Snyder.

A part of me didn't want her anywhere near the man.

But I'd promised to help her.

I grabbed my cellphone and pressed it to my ear. Bastian answered in under a second.

"How's your girl?"

"Sleeping," I said quietly. "Getting better."

"That's good."

I heard the sound of voices and a honking horn. "Where are you?"

"I told Landon I'd help him at the clinic tonight. The man totally ignores the paperwork. If it wasn't for me, he'd run the place into the ground."

Picturing Bastian in the cramped back office at Landon's clinic made me grin. "Your good guy is showing."

Bastian made a sound. "Don't insult me. I'm doing his books and investments, but there is no way I'm going near any blood or other bodily fluids."

I was silent for a moment. "It won't be much longer and she'll want to attack Snyder."

"I'm guessing she's not the pretty, sweet girl you left behind in Idaho anymore."

No, she wasn't. Instead, she was a beautiful, courageous woman who'd done everything she could to save her sister.

"She deserves her vengeance, Nash."

"I know."

"We're digging into Snyder and collating everything. When Georgie's ready, bring her into the security office. She can look over the intel. Better that she's prepared. You can't shield her from everything."

I grunted.

"I can tell you that not many people like doing business with Snyder," Bastian said. "He's a bully, habitually undercuts his suppliers, and likes to throw his weight around."

"If he does it to women, I'm not surprised he does it in his business dealings as well." Georgie shifted and I rubbed my thumb soothingly against her temple.

She was already looking more rested and relaxed after

just a few days. I wanted to keep her here forever, keeping the world away from her. But I knew that she needed her revenge.

To truly heal, she needed to know that Snyder wouldn't hurt anyone else.

"I'll bring her in when she's ready."

"Good. We'll keep gathering information. The more we have, the better we can find his weaknesses and the best spot to hit him. Then, we can help your girl take him down."

"Thanks, Bastian."

"We'll keep her safe. I've always got your back. You know that."

"I do."

"How about you take her out for dinner tomorrow? You can't keep her locked away in your villa forever."

"She might like that."

"Call Eloise at Elysium. You can have my table."

I knew that Bastian kept a private table at the restaurant. It was separate from the main floor and away from prying eyes. "I might do that."

"You can thank me later." He ended the call.

I slipped the phone away and tipped my head back against the couch. My fingers stroked Georgie's silky hair and I listened to the quiet sound of her breathing. There had been so many times over the years I would have killed for this—to be somewhere safe and comfortable, with Georgie Linden in my arms.

Now that I had her here, I never wanted to let her go.

CHAPTER 20
GEORGIE

I studied my bruises in the mirror and pulled a face.

They still looked horrible.

Okay, they were getting better. Putrid grape had been joined by some sickly-yellow. My ribs were already feeling less tender and the bullet graze on my arm was healing up nicely. I hadn't taken as many painkillers today.

And now I was going to a fancy restaurant.

Nash had told me today after our daily session at the shooting range that he was taking me to Elysium. One of the best restaurants in Las Vegas. I'd mentioned that maybe I wasn't quite ready to go out in public, but he wouldn't be swayed.

"We're going out for a nice meal. Snyder is not *stopping you from doing that."*

"You're determined to feed me."

"Yep. I won't make any apologies for that."

He'd at least promised me a quiet table in the restaurant where people couldn't see us.

A nice dinner with Nash.

I wanted that.

These last few days with him, just being together and despite everything else, had been some of the best days of my life. I brushed my hair and put it up in a simple twist. I did the best I could with my makeup. It had been so long since I'd done something nice and fun, something for myself.

Guilt pricked at me and my hands dropped, pressing to my stomach. I should be watching Snyder. Making plans to take him down.

Because of him, Viv would never do anything fun again.

Grief oozed through the guilt. I breathed through it. No, Viv wouldn't want me to stop living. She'd be the first to want me to get out there and live.

Girl, get your ass to that restaurant, enjoy that gorgeous hunk of a man, and have a glass of something fun for me.

With a towel wrapped around me, I headed out into my bedroom. Nash's room. I'd taken it over and he was sleeping down the hall, but I never forgot this room was his. The bed smelled like him, the closet was filled with his clothes. I shivered.

The kisses we'd shared... I touched my lips. I hadn't stopped thinking about them.

My heart skittered. I knew this was risky. If I let myself get too close, feel too much. If I fell for him...

No. I was old enough to separate my desire and my feelings. I was attracted to Nash. I had been since I was a teenager. I could explore that without falling in love.

All day today, I'd wanted to kiss him again, but after our early stint at the range, he'd had to work at the casino. He'd ordered me to nap and rest.

Landon had come to check on me again. The doctor

had stayed and played cards with me. He'd told me all about the clinic he ran. I liked him. I was so glad that Nash had good friends.

Even if they were retired-assassin ones.

It should scare me, knowing what Nash and his friends had done, but Nash had rescued me. Landon had treated me. And the others had promised to help me.

Strangely, the so-called bad guys seemed like the good guys.

And the well-known club owner who played the good guy, but was really the bad guy.

Sometimes, life wasn't black-and-white and didn't make sense.

I straightened. No more overthinking things. Tonight, I was having a nice dinner with Nash. For now, that was all I needed to focus on.

As I headed for the closet where my meager belongings were unpacked, I realized I had nothing nice enough to wear to a restaurant like Elysium. *Crap.* Clothes had been the last thing on my mind.

I stepped into the closet and pulled up short.

Oh. There was a dress hanging on a hanger.

It was gorgeous. I bit my lip. It was forest green, and I knew it would bring out the green flecks in my eyes. It had long sleeves and a high neck, but a sexy little keyhole cut out on the chest that would give a glimpse of skin.

And it was short. Designed to show off the legs. It was classy with a dash of sexy.

I pressed a hand to my fluttering stomach. It would also cover my bruises, but show off my mostly unscathed legs.

Nash had picked it for me.

Warmth filled my belly. I knew it wouldn't take much

to turn this simmering desire into a raging fire. It had been such a long time since I'd dated. I couldn't remember the last time I'd wanted sex, let alone had it.

And this was *Nash*.

Not the young man I'd daydreamed about. No, the rugged, tough, scary man I was getting to know now.

I pulled on my best set of bra and panties. They weren't fancy, but they were white and trimmed with pretty lace. Next, I slipped into the dress. I swished the skirt around my thighs. It fit me perfectly. Then, I found my set of gold, low-heeled sandals tucked in my suitcase. The ties wrapped up my calves.

Feeling beautiful, I walked out to the living room.

And nearly swallowed my tongue.

Nash was facing away from me and dressed in black. Black fitted pants, black button-up shirt tucked in at his narrow waist. It emphasized his broad shoulders and narrow hips. It also underscored the muscular strength of his body.

He turned. He hadn't shaved. All that scruff made him even more attractive.

His blue eyes locked on me. Slowly, lazily, he perused me from the top of my head, lingering on my hidden bruises, down my body to my legs.

"Fuck, you're beautiful."

I flushed. It was so nice to hear that. It was even nicer to actually feel it.

"You always were pretty," he said. "Now, you're flat-out beautiful."

"You scrub up well, yourself."

He closed the distance between us, and held out a hand, palm up. I put my hand in his. Then he paused, and reached out to touch my hair.

"Like starlight. Hungry?"

Strangely enough, I was. But not just for food. I nodded.

"I have something for you," he said.

He spun and picked up a single orchid off the kitchen island. A Georgiana.

"Oh." I touched the beautiful petals. "It's so soft."

"I always thought the sprinkle of dots reminded me of your freckles."

I laughed. "I hated my freckles when I was younger."

"I always thought they were beautiful. He stroked a finger down my nose. "I have a vase you can put it in."

I held the flower as he found a slim vase in a cabinet and filled it with water. I set the flower in it and smiled. "Beautiful. I still can't believe you grow such amazing orchids."

"Sometimes I can't, either." He set the vase on the counter and then took my hand. "Let's go."

He didn't let go of my hand as we headed into the casino.

I discovered that Elysium was on the top floor of one side of the large building that housed the Avernus. The doors were flanked by two green walls filled with greenery and flowers.

I sucked in a breath. I'd never seen anything like it. "This place is stunning."

Inside was more of the same. The ceiling was covered in pops of green, as were the walls. Lots of purple and white orchids were tucked in amongst the lush greenery.

"Yours?" I asked.

He nodded.

"Good evening, Mr. Oakley." A short, curvaceous woman with red hair and wide smile greeted us. She wore a beautiful bronze dress with a wide skirt. "We have your table ready."

"Thanks, Eloise."

We were ushered into a small, private nook that was shielded from the rest of the restaurant by a mass of potted greenery. Our table felt like it was nestled in the middle of the jungle. The scent of blooms mixed with the sizzling scent of meat frying.

Nash held out a chair for me.

"I have a drink for the lady." A young male server appeared. His black shirt had a touch of bronze at the collar. He was holding a fancy glass that was filled with a baby-pink liquid. "The gentleman arranged it for you."

"It's a mocktail," Nash said. "You can't have any alcohol with your painkillers."

"I'm not much of a drinker anyway." I took the glass with a smile and sipped. The drink was tart and sweet. "This is delicious."

The man nodded. "The chef will be serving you a custom tasting menu."

"That sounds great." My throat tightened as Nash sat across from me and the server disappeared. "It's been a long time since I just enjoyed myself."

He rested a big hand over mine. "You deserve it."

"I feel guilty," I whispered. "Viv's dead. She would have loved this place. She's only been gone such a short time."

"I didn't know her well, but I suspect she's the first person who'd want you to be happy."

"I know."

We chatted as the first of many courses arrived. He kept the conversation light. We talked about things that had happened during the intervening years when we'd been apart. I told him about attending the local college to study hospitality and event management. He told me a little about life in the military. He made it clear that he couldn't say much about his classified work as an assassin.

I toyed with my glass. "I waited for you to come home."

His head jerked up. We'd just finished a delightful dessert.

I gave him a small smile. "I thought when your parents died that you'd come back."

"I was doing some pretty dangerous work at the time. They were already buried by the time I found out that they'd died. I always knew they'd go close together." He touched my fingers. "I wanted to come back. I wanted to see you, even if Elliot would kick my ass from beyond the grave."

"He would not."

"He would. He warned me off you. Said you were too sweet for me."

I made an annoyed sound.

"I knew he was right."

There was a cool chill to his voice and the air lodged in my throat.

His eyes met mine, dark and churning. "I was into some pretty dark stuff. I didn't want you anywhere near that. I wasn't nice to be around."

My fingers tightened on his. "I wouldn't have cared."

"I know, but I did. I wanted you to have a good, normal life. I didn't want you dragged into what I was doing. Or worse, make you a target. I did a hard job so that you could live a good life."

I gave a soft, but harsh, laugh. "Life had other plans."

His face hardened. I tried to pull away, but he shifted

his chair back and pulled me out of my chair. He yanked me onto his lap.

"Nash—"

"Shh." He pressed his face to my hair. "Let me hold you. I'm sorry you suffered. I should've checked on you. "

"I'm not your responsibility."

He tilted my chin up. I saw the hard edges to his face. "Yeah, you are." His hand rested on my thigh and squeezed. I felt his calluses on my skin and goosebumps shivered over me.

"When you didn't come home for Elliot's funeral, I knew you were never coming back," I whispered.

His arms tightened on me. "Fuck, I miss him. He was the best of us. Good, solid, dependable." Nash chuckled. "That makes him sound like a golden retriever. He'd hate that."

He would. "I miss him too."

"I thought of you so much. Once, I was in a bad place. I'd carried out a mission, I was on the run and being hunted." His chest shuddered. "I was hiding in the attic of this barn in a village in a country I will never tell you about." He drew in a breath. "I imagined holding your hand, pulling you into my arms, kissing you. Just the memory of your smile kept me going."

Oh, God. The air lodged in my chest. I shifted on his lap and felt the hard bulge growing beneath me.

"*Nash.*" It was a needy whisper.

His hand gripped my thigh, his thumb rubbing in maddening circles.

"You're still hurt. *Nothing* is happening between us until your bruises are gone and you're fully healed."

"Nash, I'm fine—"

He shook his head, then set me on my feet.

"How about a stroll through the casino?"

I huffed out a breath. A stroll wasn't what I wanted. "Fine."

He thanked the restaurant staff, then led me to the elevators.

As we walked into the casino, he held my hand in his. He led me past a wide corridor filled with high-end stores. I glanced at the beautiful clothes in the window. I hadn't bought any nice clothes in so long. I hadn't needed them.

There were more classy, bronze Christmas decorations strung up everywhere. My heart squeezed.

"Viv loved Christmas." My first Christmas without her. My first where I'd be alone.

"Can't say I've celebrated Christmas much," Nash said.

No, I guess badass retired assassins didn't care much about Christmas.

I shoved all thoughts of the holiday out of my head. We walked through a wide doorway and onto the main casino floor.

Nash led me through the maze of tables. People were playing cards, throwing dice, shrieking in delight as they won, or groaning in disappointment as they lost. I realized that Nash wasn't watching the gambling the way I was. He was alert and assessing the security. He nodded at a man in a suit with an earpiece, who had to be staff.

We wandered on.

"You want to try some blackjack?" he asked.

I laughed. "No. Not my thing."

"Roulette?"

I shook my head. "Do you gamble?"

"Not really. I occasionally get together with Bastian and the others to play poker. Bastian always cleans us out."

We strolled on and a broad-shouldered man with blond

hair at a table caught my attention. I froze. *Oh my God*. It was Sam Alden. Snyder's thug. There was a dark-haired man beside him. Zanotti. Alden bumped a shoulder against Zanotti, the men laughing and slugging back their drinks.

All the blood drained from my face.

"Georgie? Georgie?"

All I could see in my head was these two men hurting Viv.

"Georgie."

I blinked and looked at Nash.

He cupped my cheeks. "What's wrong?"

"Snyder's men," I whispered. "Alden and Zanotti."

Nash pulled me against his chest, his big hand cupping the back of my head. His lips brushed my ear. "Zanotti's dead. I killed him."

I clung to him and remembered. I'd seen Zanotti go down. I lifted my head and looked at the blond man playing blackjack.

It wasn't Alden.

I released a shuddering breath.

Nash ran a soothing hand up and down my back. "You okay?"

I nodded. "I'm sorry."

He tilted my chin up. "You have nothing be sorry for."

"Nash, I can't wait much longer. I have to stop Snyder and the others before they hurt another woman."

His face turned serious. "I know."

Suddenly, a man's raised voice cut across the floor. A woman screamed.

I turned and saw Nash's head whip up, like a dog catching a scent.

Two men were pushing and shoving. A woman in a tiny, blue dress was scrambling out of the way.

"You cheated!" one man bellowed. "You stole my chips."

"Fuck off," the other man said. "I didn't touch anything."

"Don't speak to me like that, asshole."

It was clear they'd both been drinking.

"Stay here." Nash shoved forward.

There was no way I was staying there. I followed him. Before we reached them, one man swung a fist and connected with the other man's jaw. The victim shouted.

A scuffle broke out. A dealer stepped in, trying to de-escalate the situation, but they knocked into him and sent the man sprawling to the floor.

The pair swung around, still hitting each other, and stumbled into a trio of young women. The ladies fell in a tangle, knocking over chairs.

I watched as Nash charged in.

He grabbed one man by the back of his shirt. "Cool it."

"Screw you! Let me at him."

I watched, mesmerized, as Nash swept the man's legs out from under him. It was a fast, simple move. The man collapsed and hit the floor with an *oof*.

The second man was still riled. He rushed at Nash from behind.

"Nash!" I yelled.

He didn't need my help. Like he sensed it, he whirled, then ducked the man's sloppy punch.

Nash took a step forward, then hit the man in the back of the head. He fell forward, and hit the nearby poker table headfirst, then collapsed with a groan.

The look on Nash's face was one of total control, edged

with impatience. Leaning over, he flipped the first man onto his stomach.

"Stay down." He did the same at the second man. Then he lifted a hand and waved. I spotted security guards on their way.

Nash hadn't hesitated. He'd charged in, knowing he could handle the situation.

I shifted on my feet, energy filling me. No, it was more than that. I pressed my thighs together. I was turned on.

God. I wasn't usually one to be turned on by violence. But it wasn't the violence that got to me, it was Nash. His strength, competence.

I watched him speak briefly with the security team. Two security guards hauled the brawling men to their feet.

Then Nash looked at me.

I shifted again, trying to control my desire. His gaze narrowed on me, and I licked my lips.

CHAPTER 21
NASH

Adrenaline was pumping through me.

A part of me felt Georgie watching, and I didn't want to look at her. She'd seen the violent side of me. The darkness trained to kill.

The part of me that liked to kill.

There was a reason I was good at it. And there it was. The reason I've never gone back to Georgie. The ugliness that I knew no one, except my fellow assassins, could understand.

I didn't kill for pleasure, but taking down someone who deserved it didn't bother me one bit.

I lifted my head and my gaze locked with hers.

Then, in an instant, everything in my body froze.

Fuck. She was watching me, her eyes a little wide, her lips parted, and her cheeks flushed the prettiest pink.

There was desire in every line of her body, written all over her face.

My cock swelled, need raging through me.

My hands fisted. Hands that I'd just used to take down those assholes.

Desperately, I reminded myself that she was injured. She was still in pain and covered in bruises, her ribs sore.

I blew out a breath.

"Nash?"

Theo's deep voice made me shake my head. I turned to look at the head of security.

He raised a brow. "You okay?"

"Yeah. You've got this?"

The man glanced at Georgie then back at me. "I'll take care of things."

Georgie came toward me. "Are you okay?"

"I'm fine." I cleared my throat. "Georgie, this is Theo Garrett. He's head of the security for the Avernus."

"Hi," she said.

Theo nodded his head. "Heard you're doing really well at the shooting range." He tipped his chin toward me. "Glad you're taking good care of this guy."

"Oh, it's the opposite. He's taking care of me."

"I reckon you've got that wrong, little lady." He stepped back. "I'll take care of our troublemakers. You two go." He strode away to join the security team.

"The way you dealt with them…" Georgie grabbed my hand. "You made it look so easy."

"I'm well trained."

She shook her head. "It was more than that. It was you. Protecting people." Her hand slid up my arm. "*Nash*."

Need vibrated in her voice.

It had been building up between us all evening. Hell, it had been building up the last few days. With each stolen kiss, each moment we'd spent together. I told myself over and over that I wasn't going there, not while she was still hurt.

"*Please,*" she whispered. Then she went on her toes and kissed the underside of my jaw.

My hands clenched on her hips. She was so damn beautiful and she smelled so good.

"I need you," she murmured.

No one had ever needed me. Sure, my country had needed me to kill, but I'd just been a tool.

I wrapped my hand around hers and pulled her across the casino floor. I marched past the tables and spotted Bastian watching us, but ignored him. I slapped my hand to the lock on one of the staff doors.

It beeped and I dragged her through. The corridor was empty.

With a small sound, Georgie leaped at me. I caught her, and she wrapped her legs around my hips, her arms around my neck. Then her mouth was on mine.

I cupped her sweet ass and kissed her back.

Mine. Mine. Mine.

The words roared in my head. She rocked against me.

I cursed. I knew we were still in range of the security cameras. I'd helped plan all their locations, after all.

I carried her down the hall. There was a stairwell at the end, and I stepped sideways into a small alcove that provided a blind spot that had always bugged me. I pinned her to the wall.

"*Nash,*" she panted.

Pressing my face to her neck, I nipped at her skin, then raked my teeth over her collarbone. "I'm not fucking you, Georgie."

Her face fell and she made a pained sound. "You... don't want me?"

My low growl echoed off the walls. I pressed my lower

body against hers and knew she couldn't miss the hard line of my cock digging into her belly.

"That feel like I don't want you? The only thing I want more is *not* to hurt you. And the way I want to fuck you…" I slid one hand around her throat, rubbing her pulse point. It fluttered like a frightened bird. "I won't be in control. I won't be gentle."

Her chest hitched.

"I need you fully healed for that. No bruised face or sore ribs."

Now she pulled a face, and it made me want to smile. I rubbed my thumb over her lips.

"Doesn't mean I won't take care of you."

Her hazel eyes flicked back up and locked on mine. The green flecks stood out.

I ran a hand down her body, over the dress I picked for her, and she pushed into my touch.

"I love this dress on you. I knew the color would look amazing."

She made a husky sound.

I nudged until she dropped her legs back to the floor. My hands fisted in the fabric of her dress and I started drawing it up her legs.

She bit her lip, her eyes widening. "*Nash*. Someone could see us."

I knew this part of the corridor was rarely used, and we were tucked around a corner, but there was still a chance.

She swallowed. "Snyder…he recorded—" She broke off.

I released her dress. "You don't want anyone to see?"

She shook her head. "It's private. I just want it to be us."

I swung her into my arms and headed back down the hall. I took the next corner and stopped at a door. I pressed my palm to the lock, and it opened.

It was dark inside, with only faint floor lights illuminating the space. I walked deeper into the space, dodging around some large props.

"What is this place?" she asked.

I set her down.

"Storage room for props and sets for the stage shows in the main auditorium. Whatever isn't getting used gets kept in here." I nudged her back against the wall. Some fake vines and flowers from the Persephone show that had been held last year draped down around us. "No one comes in here." I dropped to my knees in front of her. "It's just us, Georgie. No one's going to see me giving you pleasure." I pushed the hem of her dress up, baring her slim thighs. "No one will see me with my mouth devouring your sweet pussy."

Her hands gripped my shoulders, her breathing quickening.

I uncovered a scrap of silk in the palest white. I pulled the panties down her legs, then shoved them in my pocket. "These are mine now." I pushed her thighs apart, revealing a small patch of blonde hair. There was just enough light that I could already see her folds glistening. "Oh yeah, you want my mouth between your thighs."

Her muscles clenched. "*Yes*."

Damn, I needed a taste of this woman. I'd been hungry for a taste for years. I leaned forward and buried my face against her pussy. She cried out. I discovered Georgie tasted like the sweetest honey.

"Do you know how many times I fantasied about this?" My voice was low and rough. Gripping her thighs, I lapped at her, taking my time. She pushed eagerly against my mouth. I pulled one thigh around my head. I wanted to make her come on my tongue, wanted to hear her pleasure.

"Nash, God, please. Don't stop." Her fingers tangled in my hair.

No chance in hell that I'd stop. I slid a finger into her slick heat.

"Yes." She tugged on my hair. "Deeper. Push it deeper."

I pulled out then slid two fingers inside her. Her gasping cries were so damn sweet, and my cock was so hard it was painful.

Working my fingers into her tightness, I ran my tongue over her clit, and she jerked. I sucked it into my mouth, thrusting my fingers deep.

"Nash!" Her thighs shook as she came. She cried my name again, her hands clenching in my hair.

I felt her inner muscles clutching at my fingers.

Fuck. Desire had my insides twisted, my cock in a vise. But this was for her. Nothing felt better than feeling and tasting her pleasure. I rubbed my cheek against her silky thigh.

Finally, I rose, licking my lips. "Perfect."

She sagged against me with a little laugh. "That was supposed to be my line." She sounded breathless. "That was…everything."

No, she was everything.

My everything.

I gently kissed her lips. "Come on, bedtime."

"I need my panties back."

"Nope." With an arm around her shoulders, I steered her out of the storage room.

"Nash."

I pressed a kiss to her nose. "They're mine now." Just like she was.

CHAPTER 22
GEORGIE

I woke up and smiled.

Sprawled in Nash's bed, I stretched sinuously, like a very pleased cat. It felt good to wake up and feel... Not so weighted down by dread and sorrow.

Sitting up, I noticed a fresh orchid on the bedside table, and smiled. This one had tiny flowers, white with a purple center, and was so pretty. I loved every orchid he gave me.

Two days had passed since our dinner at Elysium. Nash had been strict about me resting and healing.

I'd barely done anything, to the point that I felt lazy. He'd had food delivered every day. Last night, he'd cooked steaks on his small grill on the back patio. Other than that, I hadn't seen much of him during the last two days. His security work at the Avernus was keeping him busy, and he said he had some contract work to do at the Bellagio and the Aurora, too.

I hadn't wanted to get in his way, not when he was already doing so much for me.

He assured me that he and the others were also busy gathering intel on Dean Snyder in the meantime. He could see the wait to deal with the man was itching at me.

"The best missions are the ones where you have the most intel. The more information you have, the greater your chance of success. You've got to have patience, Georgie."

I rose and quickly headed for the bathroom to freshen up. I pulled on a pair of jeans and my favorite red T-shirt with a V-neck. I pulled my hair into a ponytail and studied my face. My bruises were so much better. The ugly yellow was fading, and I only had a small patch of dark bruising under my eye. All of it was easily covered by makeup now. My toes curled.

I was counting down the minutes until Nash touched me again.

He hadn't since that hot moment in the store room, with his mouth between my legs. I shivered, tingles running over my skin.

It had been the best orgasm of my life.

I wanted him. I wanted to explore that hard body of his. I breathed in a sharp breath. But I couldn't let myself get too attached. I had to tread very carefully.

In the living area, I saw a note propped on the kitchen island.

There's a protein shake in the fridge. Drink it.

I rolled my eyes. Even his writing sounded bossy.

I'm in the greenhouse.

He was here. My heart did a little dance in my chest. I pulled out the protein drink and poured it into a glass. I tasted berries and banana and mango. As I drank it, I wandered the living room. Nash had loads of books. The shelves were filled with varying genres—from non-fiction to thrillers. I'd spent some time reading a new crime thriller the last few days. I ran my fingers over the spines. I found the photo frame I'd discovered yesterday, tucked away at the end of the shelf. Elliot and Nash, both in their Navy uniforms, smiling at the camera. So young. They'd thought themselves invincible, that they had their entire lives ahead of them. I gently touched my brother's face. It was the only photo Nash had. I set the frame down and turned.

I'd also learned Nash loved action movies—something we shared. We'd watched the latest Jason Statham movie last night.

I'd found it hilarious that the actor was playing a retired assassin. Nash had grumpily picked it apart while I'd giggled.

I thought all I wanted, or that I could feel, was my need for vengeance. To avenge Viv's death.

But Nash had changed that. He was taking care of me, in more ways than one.

He was willing to kill for me.

He was making me want things I shouldn't.

I needed to see him. I drank the last of the protein shake and rinsed the glass in the sink. Then, barefoot, I went to find him.

It was another cool, wintery Las Vegas day. The air was fresh and the sun hid behind clouds. I followed the path to the greenhouse and moved quickly across the cool concrete. I opened the glass door and got hit by humidity and rich scents.

I pushed through the greenery and saw him. I jerked to a stop, my heart kicking against my ribs.

He was wearing jeans and no shirt. It was my favorite look on him. He was leaning over a plant, the muscles in his back flexing, and denim cupping his muscular ass.

God. I thought I'd understood desire. I'd had sex in the past, and thought it had been good sex.

Clearly, I had no clue. The depth of the heat that Nash made me feel was all-consuming.

His head whipped around, and he smiled. "Morning."

I cleared my throat. "Hey. How are your orchids?"

"Doing well."

"Do you sing to them?" I teased, wandering closer.

"No," he answered gruffly.

I really wanted to touch him, but instead, clasped my hands together.

"How do you feel today?" he asked.

"Good." I waved at my face. "Look, you can barely see the bruises."

"Ribs?" He reached for me, his hands spanning my rib cage. At his touch, I swallowed a moan.

"They feel fine."

"Good, because you have training today."

"Training?" I blinked. "At the range?" We'd been to the shooting range every day and I was pretty darn proud of how much my shooting had improved.

"Not today. Today, we'll be doing hand-to-hand. I want to show you some basic skills, so you don't get cornered. And so you can take down a bigger opponent."

That sounded good. "Okay."

He squeezed me, then let me go.

When I shifted on my feet, his eyebrow arched. "Something else?"

Life was too short. Everything that had happened had taught me that. "I want to touch you."

There was a flash in his blue eyes. "You're not ready yet."

I lifted my chin. "I'm healed."

He stared at me, and I realized his body was so tense. I blinked. *Oh God.* I stared at the taut muscles in his neck, at the way his abs were clenched. He was holding himself back.

And it wasn't easy for him.

I felt flush with power. I pressed my hands to his chest and felt his muscles flex.

"You like when I touch you," I murmured.

He was quiet for a moment. "Yeah." His voice was low and gritty.

This man—one I'd dreamed and fantasized about for so long—wanted me. He'd stood up for me when no one else had.

I spread my fingers over his bronze skin and kneaded. Explored. One finger circled his nipple and I watched it tighten.

His chest hitched and I felt a flood of damp between my legs. When I looked down, I could see the bulge of his cock behind the denim.

I stepped closer and pressed a kiss to his pec. My hand drifted lower, my fingers running over the ridges of his abs.

"Georgie…"

"Mmm." I licked his skin. God, he smelled good. Male, a woody undertone with a citrus-fresh scent on top.

I bit him and he groaned.

God, I'd wanted him when I was a young woman, but I couldn't comprehend the depth of my desire now. Body shaking a little, I let my hands move lower to the button of his jeans. The denim was stretched over a now-impressive erection.

"No." He caught my wrist.

My stomach fell. "Nash—"

"Not yet, sweetheart. But soon."

A small, needy sound escaped me. He gripped my jaw and forced me to meet his gaze. "You wet?"

Everything inside me clenched. "Yes."

"Your panties soaked for me?"

I touched my tongue to my lip. "I'm not wearing any."

Something inside him snapped. He whipped me around and I gasped. My back was pressed to his front, his hard cock rubbing against my ass.

"I'll take care of you. Suddenly, I'm starving." His hands moved, opening my jeans and he shoved them down my legs. Then, he spun and pushed me down to my knees, bending me over the bench I'd sat on the other day.

"*Nash.*" Excitement filled me.

He knelt behind me, his callused hands squeezing my ass. Then I felt his hot breath between my legs. I squirmed.

Then his mouth was on me.

My cries filled the greenhouse. I arched my back, sensation rocketing through me.

He growled loudly. The sound vibrated through me, then his tongue darted out, licking, stabbing into me. His hands gripped my waist, holding me still for his hungry assault.

"*Nash,*" I cried. "Don't stop, please don't stop."

He found my clit and sucked hard.

With a scream, I splintered apart. I was tossed into my climax and pleasure swamped me. I rode the wave until I went lax. My body slumped against the workbench and I fought for air.

"You just get more beautiful." Nash pressed a damp kiss to my buttock.

I felt like a limp dishrag. Pleasure was still singing through me.

"A girl could get used to this," I said breathlessly.

"Good." He sounded very satisfied.

I looked back over my shoulder. God, he was gorgeous. My gaze dropped to the straining erection in his jeans. "Can I touch you? I want—"

He stroked a hand down my back. "No. That was for you, sweetheart."

I huffed out a frustrated breath. "When?"

He leaned forward, grinding against me. "Soon." Then he landed a light smack to my cheek. "No time for you to laze around naked. It's time to get dressed, with panties this time. You have training today."

CHAPTER 23
NASH

UNSANCTIONED
SERIES

Twisting, I grabbed Georgie and slammed her to the mat. Still conscious of her ribs, I kept most of my weight off her.

The air rushed out of her and she glared up at me. "No fair."

"You lost focus." I pushed off her and held my hand out.

She slapped it away and rose to her feet herself. "You distracted me."

"Distracted you?" I raised a brow.

She set her hands on her hips. Her hair was in a pony-tail, but askew, and her skin was damp with perspiration. We'd been at it for over an hour in the security gym.

She was beginning to tire, but she was determined.

"Yes. You distracted me with your hard, sweaty body." She waved a hand at me.

I grinned at her. I'd changed into black work-out shorts and a fitted, compression T-shirt for our session.

She poked her tongue out and pointed at the mat. "Again?"

I nodded. I'd been showing her some moves for breaking free if an attacker grabbed her. I circled her. She was wearing black leggings and a fitted tank. I could see no bruises except the faded one below her eye.

I lunged at her. She dodged. Then she spun and launched a kick aimed for my knee.

I made a menacing noise and grabbed her. I got a hold of her arm but she twisted, stepped closer, then broke my hold with one of the moves I'd taught her.

"Good." I smiled at her.

"I was—"

I charged her. Wrapping my arms around her from behind, I lifted her off her feet. I had her arms pinned to her side.

She cursed and wriggled.

"I've got you now," I growled in her ear.

She rammed her head back.

Quickly, I leaned to the side and narrowly missed a broken nose. My hold loosened and she landed on her feet, spun, and then the minx aimed a knee at my junk.

I dodged fast, grabbing for her, but lost my balance. She gave me an extra shove, and I went down hard.

Georgie landed on top of me. She used her knees to pin my arms down. I could break free, but I didn't.

"I win." She threw her arms in the air, like a boxer who'd just won the championship bout. "Thank you, thank you."

She had a happy smile on her face, and her cheeks were flushed pink. Watching her was a hit to my chest. I loved seeing her like this.

I could lift her off me, but I let her have her moment.

Still smiling, her gaze met mine and now our eyes locked.

That ever-present desire flared.

"Looks like you two are working hard," a sardonic voice said.

I barely stopped my jerk at Bastian's voice. I hadn't heard him come in, and that wasn't like me. I looked over. He stood in the doorway with Alessio.

"I was just taking Nash down," Georgie declared.

Bastian's gaze flickered with amusement. "I see that. You're taking that man down, in more ways than one."

I rose, taking her with me. "Now, you can test your new skills."

Both her eyebrows winged up. "What?"

"You're going to fight against Bastian and Alessio. They're here because I asked them to help out."

"Oh." She rubbed her nose, looking a little nervous.

"Just remember what I showed you," I said.

She nodded.

Bastian slipped off his suit jacket, then rolled up the sleeves of his white shirt. Alessio was wearing black cargo pants and a black T-shirt that stretched across his lean chest. His tattoos were on display.

I shot them both a warning look. *Be careful with her.*

With a tilt of his head, Bastian stepped onto the mat and circled her. He smiled, full of charm. "Don't worry, we'll go easy on you, darling."

Her gaze narrowed.

I smiled. My girl wouldn't fall for the charm.

Alessio moved in the opposite direction, silent, watching her. She eyed him and shifted nervously.

Bastian sauntered closer. "You're very beautiful. I can see why you have our man tied up in knots."

I swallowed a growl. I didn't need Bastian commenting

on how beautiful she was. I wanted him focused on training her.

Suddenly, he lunged. Shit, he was just distracting her.

But Georgie wasn't fooled.

She turned with him and grabbed his shirt. I saw surprise register on his face. Then she hooked her ankle around his and yanked.

Bastian didn't go down, he was too good for that, but he did stumble.

She shoved him and leaped back, well out of range.

Instantly, she looked for Alessio.

The other man rushed her. He grabbed her arm, tugged her closer, then got her in a hold from behind.

She lifted her legs, and he staggered under the added weight. They went down on the mat, and I took a step forward. I didn't want her getting hurt.

Plus, I really didn't like seeing another man half on top of her.

She didn't pause. She kicked at Alessio—who turned to protect himself—and she rolled free.

When she rose, she grinned.

"Nice work, sweetheart." Pride welled inside me. I walked toward her.

She was glowing. "I kicked ass."

"You did." I kissed the tip of her nose.

"Because of you." She grabbed my hand. "Thank you, Nash."

She was thanking me for walking her to the dark side. I still wasn't sure how I felt about that.

But this was Georgie. *My Georgie.*

I'd do anything for her.

"Well, I guess we lost." Bastian crooked a finger. "Time for a do-over."

Georgie straightened. "What?"

I nodded. "Go again."

She set her shoulders back. "All right, let's do this."

Bastian and Alessio attacked.

She didn't win all of the next attacks, but she was doing well. She landed on the mat several times, but she also broke free of their holds a lot. She listened to what I was teaching her. She learned from the guys.

By the end, I saw that she was tired and favoring her side. "Okay, let's leave it there. Good work, Georgie." I handed her a bottle of water.

She gulped it down gratefully.

I could tell Bastian and Alessio were both impressed.

Bastian smiled, re-tucking his shirt. "You did very well, Georgie. That means I should buy you dinner."

She smiled. "I think so."

I scowled. "Buy *us* dinner."

My friend smirked. "Of course. That's what I meant."

CHAPTER 24
GEORGIE

UNSANCTIONED
SERIES

B astian's penthouse was mind-blowing. I felt very much like a small-town girl as I walked inside.

It had a dark, moody vibe—black with bronze accents like the main casino—that was very masculine and screamed wealth. The floor was a glossy, black marble with bronze veins through it, the furniture was black and sleek.

Viv would have loved this place. My heart squeezed. God, I missed her.

Nash seemed comfortable in the space. He headed straight for the built-in fridge in the slick kitchen. There was an enormous island, with modern, bronze pendant lights hanging over it. I had a sneaking suspicion the fancy appliances cost more than my car.

Alessio sat at the long table that had a million chairs. It was the longest dining table I'd ever seen.

"I ordered from Sinatra," Bastian said from behind the island.

Named after the famous singer, I'd heard of the well-known Italian restaurant in the Wynn Casino. "Sinatra does take out?"

Bastian smiled that slow smile I knew must charm the panties off the ladies. "No. But they do for me. I hope you worked up an appetite, Georgie."

Nash edged closer to me, his body crowding mine.

"Beer or wine?" Bastian asked.

"She's still on painkillers," Nate grumbled. "She'll have a soda."

I pulled a face. "A soda would be great."

Bastian waved at the giant fridge. "Take your pick."

I nabbed a Diet Coke and Bastian handed me a glass with some ice. The front door of the penthouse opened and Cole strode in, shrugging off a leather jacket. My gaze dropped to his muscular arms and the tattoos snaking up the left one.

"Where's dinner?" he asked.

"Coming, you heathen." Bastian tossed Cole a beer.

Cole spotted me and nodded.

"Hi, Cole."

"I'm gonna help out with your training, too." His voice was low, raspy. "Heard you're doing well."

I fought a flush of pleasure. "Thank you."

Right now, Cole didn't look like he was retired from anything. His knuckles were all torn up.

Landon breezed in. "Hi. Hey, Georgie." He leaned over and touched my face. "The bruises are almost gone."

"Finally."

"How are your ribs?"

"As good as new. I started hand-to-hand combat training today."

"She held Alessio and me off several times," Bastian said. "She has good instincts."

I couldn't hold back my pleasure at the praise. Beside me, Nash tugged on my ponytail, and I saw pride on his face.

The doorbell rang.

"That's the food." Bastian sauntered toward the door.

Before I knew it, I was sitting at the table with these gorgeous, dangerous men, gorging on pizza and pasta. Nash sat beside me and kept putting food on my plate.

I leaned closer to him. "You're going to give me a complex. Clearly, you think I'm too thin."

He slid an arm across the back of my chair. "I know you haven't been taking care of yourself. But you're beautiful no matter what." He lowered his voice. "I think I've shown my appreciation of your body several times."

"Not as much as I'd like," I muttered.

He reached over and touched the fading bruises beside my eye. "Soon."

I shivered.

"Cole, I heard you fought like a machine last night." Bastian sipped his glass of wine. "I won good money on you."

Cole just grunted.

"Are you a boxer?" I asked. That would explain the knuckles, although I knew boxers normally wore gloves.

Nash shook his head. "Cole takes part in underground fights. The rules are...more fluid. Anything goes."

My eyes widened. "Oh." That had to be dangerous.

Cole lifted a shoulder. "I like fighting. I'm good at it."

He definitely hadn't been in the military, like Nash. He didn't give off that vibe at all. I wondered what demons drove him to fight in the ring.

"How's the clinic?" Nash asked Landon.

"Busy."

The conversation ebbed and flowed. They were all so comfortable with each other. Low male laughter echoed around the table. They weren't afraid to tease each other. I wondered if my family had ever shared meals like this? If we had, I couldn't remember it. My heart squeezed.

Nash and his friends looked out for each other. They were family.

I was glad Nash had that.

No wonder he hadn't come home. He hadn't needed to.

And now, I'd brought more trouble to his door. More death. I'd dragged him back into killing, something that he'd left behind.

I gnawed on my bottom lip. After this was over, after we burned off this attraction, what would I do?

I guessed I'd leave. Nash had a life he liked, work he was good at, and friends.

I swallowed. I had nothing. A degree I'd never used. No job. No home.

God, did he think I was using him?

Suddenly, I needed to move, to do something. I rose and started to stack the dirty plates.

"Leave it, Georgie," Bastian said.

"No, it's fine. I don't mind." I grabbed the plates and headed for the kitchen. I needed to escape.

I felt Nash's gaze burning between my shoulder blades.

I stacked the dirty plates in Bastian's fancy dishwasher. Once I was done, I glanced up and spotted a small balcony off the kitchen, the glimmer of the Las Vegas lights outside. I slid open the glass door and slipped outside.

The air was cold and the wind whipped at me. I breathed deeply and wrapped my arms around my middle. The lights below were a blur. Honking horns and the thump of music from somewhere close combined into a strange melody.

I just needed to stay focused on Snyder. On revenge. On avenging Viv. My hands curled on the railing.

I couldn't risk getting too attached to Nash. I had to keep my heart locked up safely.

I didn't hear the door, so I jolted when I sensed someone behind me.

"Sorry. Didn't mean to startle you." Bastian leaned an elegant hip against the railing beside me.

"I needed some fresh air."

"You won't have long before Nash realizes you're missing."

I glanced at him. "I'm not using him."

Bastian turned to rest his elbows on the railing, his gaze on my face. The wind ruffled his thick hair. "I never suggested that."

"I...I came here with nothing but problems. He's taking care of me, helping me. He deserves someone way more together than me. He has all of you, he has a good life."

"He deserves what makes him happy."

"He's going to kill for me. Kill again. The thing that he left behind."

"He wants to help you. He'd do anything for you."

I blew out a breath.

"You know he carries a photo of you in his wallet. The girl he never forgot. I think you give him far more than you realize, Georgie." With that, Bastian slipped inside, leaving me churning with conflicted emotions.

CHAPTER 25
NASH

UNSANCTIONED
SERIES

fter she'd returned from the kitchen, Georgie had been quiet. I kept an eye on her, worried she'd overdone it today.

The guys were all having a bourbon. I swirled mine around my glass, glancing at her.

Maybe it was just fatigue, but she looked like she was thinking about something.

Someone's phone beeped, and it was Bastian who pulled his cellphone out. He frowned, then caught my gaze.

I stiffened. "What?"

"The security team I have watching Snyder's club sent some photos."

Beside me, Georgie straightened. "I want to see."

Bastian was still and silent for a moment, then he nodded. He rose and strode into the living area. It was dominated by a curved, black couch and the huge TV on the wall. He tapped on his phone and the TV flared to life.

I wondered if Bastian ever just sat and watched television.

The others walked over, too, and I stood behind Georgie.

Photos appeared on the screen, taken with a telephoto lens. Snyder, Bruno, and a few of his other goons were entering the club. They were laughing.

Tension wafted off Georgie. She stared at the screen.

The next photo showed a sleek BMW sedan pulling up. A woman exited the vehicle.

Georgie sucked in a breath. "She went back." She squeezed her eyes closed. "That idiot. She's Viv's replacement. A singer. Her name's Shandy."

"Snyder is good at manipulation," Bastian said quietly. "He's holding her dreams in his hand. That's a powerful temptation."

Georgie leaned back against me. Her hand reached back and gripped my thigh, her fingers digging in. I wrapped my arm around her.

"The next photos are after the club closed," Bastian said carefully.

Hell. I knew that tone. It wasn't going to be good.

I saw Snyder hauling the woman outside. I stiffened. *Fuck.*

Georgie stiffened too, her body turning to steel.

Shandy's lipstick and mascara were smudged. Her lips were swollen, her dress askew. There were bruises on her arms.

She'd been crying.

I didn't need three guesses to know what had happened to her.

"It's happening again."

The dull pitch to Georgie's voice made my attention snap to her. I saw the pain and grief on her face. She wasn't seeing Shandy, she was seeing Viv.

"I can't save her. I can't do anything." Her hands balled into fists.

I spun her to face me. "We *will* stop him."

Bastian and the others nodded.

"Together," Bastian said.

But Georgie couldn't hear them. She was staring, distraught, at the woman on the screen.

"Georgie?" I pressed my hand to her shoulder.

"It doesn't matter how I fight, how hard I try, people get hurt. I lose the people I love." She tried to pull away. "Mom died, Elliot died, Dad died, Viv died. I've tried so hard to be strong." She shook her head. "I haven't cried since Elliot's funeral. I just...I can't..."

I grabbed her shoulders. "You don't have to be strong every second of the day, Georgie. You aren't alone anymore."

She stared up at me with the saddest eyes.

"I've got you. Let it go."

A sob escaped her.

She broke.

Losing her sister, being hurt, everything she'd been through...she'd been strong for so long. Her legs gave way, and I caught her and hauled her close.

"Nash," she sobbed. "You should tell me to go." Tears ran down her cheeks. "You don't need my troubles."

"Shh." I nodded at the guys and they dispersed.

Lifting her, I carried her to Bastian's couch. I sat and settled her on my lap.

"I'm *never* letting you go," I told her.

She buried her face in my neck and cried. Gut-wrenching, painful sobs, like her heart was broken.

I'd give anything to stop those tears.

"It's okay, sweetheart. It's going to be okay." I'd make it

okay. Snyder was a dead man walking. "Cry. Let it all out. I'm here."

Her body shook as she wept, and I felt every bit of her grief and pain.

Finally, the tears slowed down. I rubbed my hand up and down her back. The crying stopped. I stroked her hair, and eventually, ever so slowly, she relaxed.

"I'm sorry," she whispered.

"You never have to be sorry for feeling, Georgie."

She pressed her face to my neck again.

"You've been holding a lot in." I felt damn glad she felt safe enough with me to let it all go. I rose, holding her securely in my arms.

Bastian appeared. "Get her to bed. She needs some sleep."

I nodded. "We'll meet tomorrow." I glanced at the now empty TV. "And plan exactly how and where we're going to take Snyder down. We can't wait any longer."

Bastian nodded. "We'll all be there."

I'd prefer Georgie not be involved, but I knew that she needed this. She needed to avenge her sister, and help stop any more women from getting hurt.

I carried her to the elevator.

She stirred. "I can walk."

"I don't care. I'm carrying you."

Soon, I was letting us into my villa. Darkness and shadows filled the space, and I didn't turn any lights on.

I set her down in my bedroom, just the dappled silver light coming through the window. I found one of my T-shirts, and like a robot, she shed her clothes. I pulled my shirt over her head.

"Go brush your teeth."

She didn't take long. She came back with her face clean

and smelling minty fresh. She crawled into the bed. I leaned over and stroked her hair, then straightened to leave.

Her hand grabbed mine. "Nash… Please. Stay."

Damn. I couldn't say no to her.

I stripped my shirt and jeans off, leaving my boxer briefs on. I slid into the bed beside her, and pulled the covers over us.

She turned into me, curling into my body. I kept her close and slid an arm snugly around her. "I've got you."

She let out a sigh. It was only minutes before she fell asleep.

I closed my eyes and breathed in the smell of her, absorbed the feel of her. My cock was half hard. Sleeping beside her, having her pressed against me, would be torture.

A torture I'd endure for her, to make sure she slept, and the nightmares stayed away.

CHAPTER 26
GEORGIE

"Wow, this place looks like it's out of a spy movie."

The high-tech security room at the Avernus was right next to the shooting range and gym we'd been training in. All the walls were covered in screens, each one depicting a different view of all areas of the casino—gaming tables, slot machines, restaurants, auditoriums, elevators. Nash nodded at the security people seated at the computers and pressed a hand to my lower back to lead me into a conference room.

I'd woken up alone this morning. I wished I could have woken up in his arms.

I wanted him. *Badly*.

I knew I should be solely focused on my revenge, but I couldn't ignore the feelings I had for him. This wasn't just a childhood crush anymore. I had strong, deep feelings for Nash.

That scared me.

Just like my breakdown last night had. I'd known there was a lot of grief locked inside me. But seeing that Snyder was hurting another woman like he had Viv had just knocked things loose.

That, and knowing Nash would be there to hold me. Keep me steady.

What would I do when this was over? When I had to leave?

"Good morning, Georgie." Bastian strode in, wearing another tailored suit that looked expensive. He must have a large collection of them.

"Hi." Embarrassment briefly flickered through me. He'd witnessed me breaking down last night, but he didn't mention it or act any differently.

The conference room walls were also fully covered in screens. These ones, however, were all filled with images of Snyder and his men. My stomach did a sickening turn. Just looking at him made me feel nauseated. In addition, there were also pictures of the Red Neon, his ostentatious Tuscan-style mansion, him at parties. I also saw lots of what looked like financial statements.

"This is everything my team has pulled together on Snyder." Bastian swiped at one of the screens and more data appeared. "We've been going over it and planning."

I dropped into one of the chairs. A picture of Shandy appeared on one screen. I stared at her. That poor woman.

I needed to save her before she ended up like Viv.

"Her real name is Beth Davis," Bastian said softly. "She's from a small town in Minnesota."

God. Another young woman in over her head and dazzled by Snyder's bullshit. The final screen displayed several pictures of other women, as well.

"Who are they?"

Beside me, Nash stiffened. "It doesn't matter."

"Nash." I touched his hand, then rose. I needed to

know. I looked at a very young, beautiful blonde who reminded me of Viv. I touched the screen and swiped.

The next picture showed the woman in a bathtub, her hand dangling over the side, her skin a sickly white.

I sucked in a sharp breath and spun. I knew she was dead. "Tell me."

Nash released a breath. "Viv wasn't the first."

I'd suspected as much, but actually seeing the proof that another innocent woman had died sent a cutting pain slicing through me. It hurt so badly. "How many? How many has he killed?"

"We found five others over the last four years," Bastian said, his tone somber.

"Oh, God." I dropped back into the chair. Nash shifted and knelt beside me. He grabbed my limp hand in his.

"Georgie—"

"We have to stop him," I whispered furiously. "We can't just keep waiting." Resolve filled me. "He *has* to be stopped."

Nash nodded. "He does."

"Okay." I took a deep breath, trying to get a handle on my roiling emotions.

"We'll all comb through the intel we have," Bastian said. "We need to find a way to get to Snyder and his men. Somewhere where we can take them down safely, without any collateral damage."

I swallowed. Nash pushed the laptop toward me.

"I'm also scouring his financials." Bastian's smile was scary. "I'm going to start dismantling his businesses."

I suspected having Bastian as an enemy was not a good thing. I made myself focus on the laptop and pored over the information. When I saw just how much money Snyder made, I felt sick. There were more pictures of him, at parties and events with celebrities and local personalities. Hell, in one he was winning some kind of local award.

He didn't have a care in the world.

My jaw tightened.

Nash's hand pressed to the back of my neck and squeezed. "Relax."

"It's hard when I see this…evil man living the high life, making all this money, and doing whatever he wants, no matter who he hurts. Do you know that he ran another club out of business?" I stabbed a finger at the information on the screen. "All because they opened up a block away from his club."

Nash watched me steadily.

"And one family-run supplier tried to sue him for shortchanging their payments, but he forced them into bankruptcy. He's rotten to the core."

Nash's fingers rubbed soothingly. "I told you, we're going to stop him. Soon, he won't be able to hurt anyone else."

Bastian called him over. With a nod, Nash moved to the other end of the table. I watched the pair of them. Elegant, stylish Bastian and rough, tough Nash. I focused on him. The blue light from the screens highlighted the dips and planes of his face.

Knowing I had him on my side made everything better.

Don't get attached, Georgie.

He'd walked away from me once before, and he had a good life here in Vegas.

I sucked in a breath. I knew that life could change in an instant. I knew how it felt to have the people you loved, on whom you depended, wrenched away.

God. I swallowed. I could so, so easily fall for him.

And if he left or was taken away, it would be a loss I wouldn't survive. My heart was already cracked and held together by delicate threads.

I wasn't sure I could handle any more heartache and loss.

I focused back on the laptop, but the screen was just a blur. I needed my full attention on Dean Snyder.

Some information caught my gaze. "It says here Snyder is having a special event at his club tonight. Supposedly raising money for charity." I rolled my eyes. "There's going to be a special performance by Shandy." I looked up at them. "We've got to go. We've got to protect her."

The men traded a glance.

Nash nodded his head. "We might be able to find out more information. Talk to some of the staff. Find out more about Snyder's movements."

Bastian crossed his arms and nodded. "It's not a bad idea. I'd like to see Snyder up close and personal, myself."

Nash's gaze pinned me like a laser. "You're going to stay here."

I rose and pressed my hands to the table. "Not a chance in hell."

"He could recognize you."

"I've been in there before. I'll wear a wig and a disguise. He won't expect me to be there."

"Georgie," Nash growled.

"I'm coming. Besides, I'll have several former assassins by my side. I'm safer with you than anywhere else."

Bastian cleared his throat. "She has a point."

"Fuck," was Nash's only response.

CHAPTER 27
NASH

Georgie was a ball of nervous tension beside me.

We were sitting in the back of one of Bastian's black Range Rovers, heading to Red Neon.

Bastian was in the front seat with the driver. Cole and Alessio were in the very back seat behind us. Landon couldn't get away because the clinic was swamped.

Learning as much as possible about our target was vital. I just hadn't wanted Georgie to come. But she'd given me that stubborn look. At least she was wearing a wig, and didn't look anything like her usual self. She'd told me that she'd been into the club in disguise a few times, and no one had recognized her.

Still, I didn't like it, but I knew that if I left her behind, she would just turn up anyway.

Bastian's driver pulled up across from the club.

"Thanks, Mitch." Bastian exited, tugging on the hem of his jacket. He was wearing a dark navy suit that screamed "I'm rich." Alessio was in a suit as well—his was black. Cole was wearing a black button-down shirt and dark jeans. I had on dark pants and a gray button-down shirt that I'd left open at the collar.

I held the door open for Georgie.

She was wearing a long coat in deference to the cool night, but once she exited the car, she slipped it off. I hissed in a breath.

The dress was gold. And there wasn't much to it.

It was short, shiny like liquid gold, and crisscrossed around her neck in complicated straps. The wig she wore was black, but it was a different one than the first one I'd seen her in. This one was longer, with curls that brushed her shoulders. She'd gone bold with the makeup again. Glittering gold covered her eyelids, her lashes were thick and dark, and her lips were pink.

She looked gorgeous.

"Where did you get that?" I asked.

"The stores at the Avernus. I needed something new to wear."

I grabbed her hand. "You could stay in the SUV and wait for us."

"No." She sank enough strength into the word that I knew it wasn't worthwhile arguing.

Keeping her hand in mine, we strode across the street toward the entrance. Bastian ignored the long line and headed straight for the bouncers. His stride was loose-limbed and confident.

As they saw us coming, the pair of bouncers straightened. I knew they had a radar for money and power.

"We heard this place was good." Bastian pulled out a wad of hundred-dollar bills. He discreetly handed some over.

"You're absolutely right," Thug One said. "Best club in Las Vegas. Come in, come in."

Georgie held my arm as we breezed inside.

I found the interior dark and obvious, but there was a large crowd. A redheaded hostess in a slim, black dress appeared. "Hello, welcome to Red Neon. We have a VIP couch arranged for you."

Bastian dazzled her with a smile. "Excellent. And we're going to need your best bourbon. The entire bottle."

Her eyes gleamed, no doubt calculating her tip. "Of course, Mr....?"

"Thorne."

"Mr. Thorne." She inclined her head. "This way."

She led us to a cordoned-off semicircular couch in vibrant red. Dancers were gyrating to the music on the dance floor. The bars were busy.

Georgie leaned in close. "His office is through there." She nodded her head at one wall behind us.

A door was marked Private.

"I'll take a look around," Alessio murmured.

"I'll join you." Cole followed him and they melted into the crowd.

Bastian sat on the couch, crossing his legs, looking like a king. Nearby, I saw several women eyeing him. A server in a tiny red skirt and strapless top brought the bottle of bourbon and glasses over.

I sat as well and pulled Georgie down beside me.

"The place is popular."

She nodded. "Viv was so excited to sing here." She sighed. "I wish I could go back and keep her away somehow."

I slid my arm around her. "Could haves never help. They just drive you crazy." I knew that. I'd lost fellow SEALs and agents who'd been good friends. I'd always questioned what I could've done differently. It didn't change anything.

Georgie nodded.

"There are definitely drug deals going on," Bastian murmured, as he sipped his drink.

Georgie jolted and looked around. "You can see that?"

He shook his head. "No, my team hacked the CCTV system. He's letting it happen."

My jaw tightened. Yeah, the more I learned around Snyder, the happier I was to put him down.

Alessio and Cole reappeared. Cole was holding a beer and Alessio held a glass of something clear, that I knew was soda water. The man rarely drank.

"Nine o'clock," Alessio murmured.

I swiveled and spotted Shandy the singer. Snyder was with her. He was practically dragging her toward the stage.

She tried to say something to him, but he shook his head, and shoved her.

Shandy took the stage, a forced smile on her face. The music died down, and the lights gleamed off the blue sequins of her long, slinky dress.

"Good evening." She cleared her throat. "We're all here for a special event, raising money for an excellent charity that helps the disadvantaged here in Las Vegas."

There was a smattering of applause and a few whistles.

"Now, I have a few songs for you."

The music swelled and the crowd whistled.

She started to sing. She had a hell of a voice. Soon, she was clutching the microphone and was lost in the song.

Snyder watched her with a smile. Bruno appeared at his side.

"I want to drag her off there," Georgie whispered fiercely.

"We'll get her free. Soon."

Georgie twisted her hands together. "How much damage will Snyder inflict in the meantime?"

I hugged her closer. "Stay strong. She'll be alive. That's what counts."

Georgie grabbed my hand and nodded.

Soon, Shandy had finished her set, to fervent applause. I watched Snyder hustle her into his office, along with a heavyset guy in a suit, and Bruno. Bruno was staring at Shandy's ass.

"The big guy is one of Snyder's business partners," Bastian murmured.

Georgie's devastated face said what we all knew. That Shandy would suffer behind that door.

The music from the DJ was pumping again. There wasn't a spare inch on the dance floor.

I caught Alessio's gaze. "Can you find a way to help the singer without tipping Snyder off?"

Alessio nodded. "I'm on it."

"I'll try and talk with a few bartenders," Cole said.

Bastian nodded. "I'll talk with the hostess."

I stood. "Come on." I pulled Georgie up. She needed a distraction, or she'd just sit there and worry.

"Where are we going?" she asked.

"To dance."

Her eyes widened. "You dance?"

"No, but I will for you."

Now her face softened.

The crowd parted for me as I pulled her into the throng. I found a space and pulled Georgie close, flush against my chest.

She was tense, but she slid her arms around my neck and pressed into me.

I pressed my mouth to her ear. "Just listen to the music."

Holding her close, I swayed to the music. I didn't dance, but holding her was no hardship. She started to move, her face pressed to my chest.

"Just feel," I told her.

Damn, I felt every inch of her against me. Every move, every brush, sent sensation through me. She slowly relaxed, and I pressed my face to her hair and wished she wasn't wearing that damn wig. My hands drifted down and cupped her ass.

She shivered against me and tipped her head back. Those pink lips beckoned, and I lowered my head. I took my time, kissing her, exploring every inch of her mouth. Desire kept growing, arcing between us.

These days with her...it felt like she'd brought me back to life. Being with her had injected energy and emotion into everything.

I slid a thigh between her legs and although I couldn't hear it over the music, I knew a breathy sound escaped her lips.

She tugged my head down. "Nash..."

"Mmm?"

"Don't stop kissing me."

"Yes, ma'am."

Sliding my hands up her body, I cupped her cheeks, looking deep into her eyes. She stared at me, hunger reflected back. I lowered my mouth to hers again, the hot kiss hardening my cock. Her fingernails bit into my arms, her body rocking against mine.

"I love that you're so hard," she breathed between kisses.

"And I love that you're soft and sweet." All I could feel was her: her heat, her taste, the way she pressed into me.

A sudden blaring noise ripped through the club. I froze, and she jolted.

It was a fire alarm.

I pulled her close, mouth to her ear. "Alessio found a way to help Shandy."

She bit her lip, relief shining in her eyes.

The crowd started to push toward the exits.

I wrapped my arm around her shoulders and kept her close. "Let's get out of here."

CHAPTER 28
GEORGIE

We were back in the Range Rover.

The men were talking about the club and Snyder and his men. But I couldn't focus.

Nash was beside me, his thigh pressed against mine.

I was wired. Desire was electric inside me, need filling every space. I liked knowing we'd been right under Snyder's nose and he hadn't known. I liked knowing that at least for tonight, Shandy was safe.

All of that was thanks to Nash.

I needed him more than I'd ever needed anything.

This was so dangerous. I'd vowed never to love again, never to get attached. Having sex with him would forge bonds. I knew that deep in my gut.

"The hostess told me that Snyder is planning a huge party at his house this week," Bastian said. "A spectacle with performers, acrobats, and fireworks."

"Could be a good place to hit him," Cole mused from the back.

"There'll be lots of guests, though," Nash added.

I pulled in a breath, trying to concentrate on what they

were talking about. Nash's muscular thigh shifted, and I almost moaned out loud.

I felt his stare and glanced up. *God*. My stomach filled with heat.

There was desire all over his rugged face—raw, primal.

The rest of the drive was a blur. I kept shifting in my seat. Finally, we pulled into the back entrance to Avernus, near the villas.

"I'll look into this party Snyder is planning," Bastian said. "Find out all the details. This could be our best bet for taking him down."

"Thanks," Nash replied.

"See you all tomorrow." Cole lifted a hand, then disappeared into the darkness.

Alessio just nodded and started to turn.

I grabbed his jacket. "Alessio?"

He glanced at me, his eyes dark and piercing.

"Thank you. For the fire alarm. For helping her."

"You're welcome." He glanced at Nash, then headed for his villa.

I focused on getting to Nash's villa, all the while feeling the heat radiating off him as he walked right beside me. We didn't touch. We didn't talk.

Inside, he disarmed the alarm, turned on the light in the entry, then dumped his keys on a small side table. Then, he reached for the panel and reset the security system.

"You want a drink?" He left the living room lights off. I watched his shadowy form as he poured what I guessed was a bourbon.

"No." I was burning up. Meanwhile, he looked cool, calm. I pulled the wig off my head and dropped it on the table. I shook my own hair free.

Then he lifted his glass and knocked the bourbon back in one long swallow. He set the glass down, moved to the couch, and dropped down on it.

"Thanks for taking me tonight."

"You would have gone anyway," he said dryly.

"Probably."

We stared at each other across the space.

"Come here." His voice was low, dark.

Everything inside me felt alive, aching. I kicked off my shoes and walked toward him. The rug was soft beneath my bare feet. He was just a dark silhouette.

My knees bumped his. "No more waiting, Nash."

"Is my Georgie hungry?"

"Nash—"

His arm snapped out and he yanked me onto his lap.

I gasped, my dress riding up as I straddled him. His hands glided up my arms, setting off goosebumps across my skin. Then he grabbed the straps of my dress and pushed them down, baring my breasts. I gasped again.

"I'm going to take care of you, sweetheart. I promise."

Then he leaned forward and his mouth closed on my nipple. I cried out. As he lapped and sucked, I slid my hands into his hair.

He nipped at the curve of my breast and I gasped. "So damn beautiful." He sucked my swollen nipple back into his mouth. When he had me writhing, he moved onto my other breast. Soon my nipples were hard pebbles, my breasts swollen. His beard scraped over my skin, spreading sensation and goosebumps all over me.

I rocked on him and felt his cock beneath me. Hard as steel.

His mouth popped free of my breast, then his lips were

on mine. The kiss was hard, wild. Our tongues stroked, and then I bit his bottom lip.

With a growl, he tumbled me onto the couch, then lifted me onto my hands and knees on the leather.

"I dream about this ass." He pushed my dress up. His big hand squeezed my cheek. He pulled on my thong and I moaned.

"And all the things I want to do to it."

The leather squeaked as he moved. With a tug, he tore the thong free. Then he pushed my cheeks apart and his mouth was on my pussy.

"*Nash.*" I dropped down to my elbows and shoved my body back against him. My cheek pressed to the cool leather.

Meanwhile, between my legs, his mouth and tongue were hot. He licked and nibbled, his tongue swirled around my clit.

I made small, husky cries, my hands gripping the leather. I could feel everything inside me tightening.

"No. You're not coming on my tongue this time, pretty girl."

He hauled me up beside him on my knees. I knew I must look like a disheveled mess with my dress bunched around my waist.

"You're coming on my cock," he ordered.

"*Yes.*" My hair tumbled loose around my shoulders. I reached for him, my hands gripping his shirt. I couldn't *not* touch him. I wanted skin. I pulled and the buttons flew everywhere.

He made a hungry sound, and I smoothed my hands over that gorgeous, hard chest.

"Take my cock out, Georgie."

The command shot through me, arrowing between my

legs. I attacked his belt and opened his pants, then I delved into his boxer shorts. In the next second, I had his long, thick cock hot in my hands. I made a sound deep in my throat and stroked him.

"That's all for you, sweetheart." His voice was guttural. "It's always hard for you."

"I want it. I want you."

I shifted back and lowered my head. Then I licked him.

He uttered a curse, his hand spearing into my hair.

Moaning, I licked the head of his cock again, tasting his salty musk. Hot, liquid desire melted through me. I swallowed the swollen head into my mouth.

"God, that feels good." The hand in my hair clenched hard. I looked up and saw him holding it out of the way so he could watch me. "Look at you. Lips stretched around my cock."

My moan vibrated on his erection, and he cursed again. I bobbed, sucking hard. His hand twisted and I felt the sting on my scalp. I loved what I was doing to him.

"Enough." He pulled me off him, lifting me.

"No," I protested.

Then I was straddling him. *Oh.* I licked my lips. This was good.

He pushed my thighs apart and stroked between them. Rough fingers swiped through my dampness. "Now, I'm filling you with my cock."

I made a sound. It was what I'd wanted forever.

"You on birth control?"

I nodded.

"I'm not using a condom. It's just you and me. I'm clean. I promise, I'll always protect you."

I nodded again. "I haven't had sex in a really long time. I've always been careful."

He urged me up onto my knees. Together, we placed his cock so the head notched between my legs. My body trembled.

Then his big hands clamped to my hips and he pushed me down. "Take me."

Slowly, I slid down on his thick cock. I gasped. It had been a long time, and I felt the sting as my body stretched to accommodate him. He felt enormous.

"*Fuck*." The muscles in his jaw were tense. He paused for a second. "So damn tight. I can't believe I'm sinking inside my Georgie. Dreamed of this."

I gripped his shoulders, panting. I continued pushing down, taking more of him. Finally, I had every inch inside me.

I met his gaze and lifted my hips.

We held there for a second, then he shoved me down. I moaned, his cock driving deep inside me. Soon, I was riding him, moving up and down. The deep groans from his chest were music to me.

"Get there, sweetheart. God, I love watching you take me." His gaze was hooded, desire on his face. Then his big hands shifted down my belly. He touched where his cock stretched me wide.

"Prettiest sight I've ever seen. Georgiana Linden taking me, pussy stretched around my cock."

I cried out his name, moving faster. So much emotion was storming through me.

Then he found my clit and rubbed.

Electric sensations hit hard. I moved even faster.

"Go over," he ordered. "On me, for me." With another circle of his thumb, I flew apart.

I arched, Nash's cock deep inside me.

My head fell back and pleasure—hot and violent—

overtook me as I cried out his name.

CHAPTER 29
NASH

uck. I was close to coming.

Watching Georgie find her release, feeling her inner muscles squeezing the life out of my cock, pushed me right to the edge.

I never fully lost control in bed. Control had been a cornerstone of my life for so long, and I never forgot that I was bigger, stronger, and trained to kill.

But holding onto that control was an impossibility with Georgie.

With a growl, I gripped her and rose to my feet. She cried out, clutching me with her arms and legs. Without losing our connection, keeping my cock deep inside her, I dropped to my knees on the rug. I laid her on her back and covered her with my body.

Damn, it was the most beautiful thing I'd seen. Georgie under me, taking my cock, the strands of her starlight hair spread around her head, and her body flushed with pleasure.

Everything inside me tightened—gut, chest, balls—and I pulled back, then shoved deep.

She cried out my name. My hips pistoned, our bodies slapping together.

"*Georgie*," I groaned.

"Don't stop." Her nails raked down my back. "I want it all."

On my next thrust, she started coming again. A second later, my climax hit like a high-impact blast. I slammed into her one last time and started coming inside her.

"*Yes*," she cried.

"So fucking good," I groaned. "And all mine."

"Yes," she panted. "Mark me."

Fuck, yes. Primal instinct took over. I pulled out, gripped my cock, and jerked. My come splattered her breasts, her belly, the top of her sex.

Spent, I fell forward, slapping my palms to the rug to stop from crushing her.

I felt drained. As though my soul had been ripped from me.

Then, Georgie smiled up at me. Sweet and flushed. As I watched, she ran her hand through my come, across her breasts, rubbing it on her skin.

"My sexy Georgie." I lowered my head and took her mouth. It was a lazy kiss. We were both sweaty and sticky. When I pulled back, I saw her eyelids flicker closed. She was tired.

I scooped her up off the floor and headed for my bedroom. "Shower, then bed."

She made a cute humming noise, then buried her face in my neck.

My cock, which should've been done, twitched.

In the bathroom, I turned the shower on and set her down inside. Soon, we were both in the steam-fogged stall under the fall of warm water. I squeezed shower gel onto my hand, then smoothed it over her body. She leaned into me. I stroked her shoulders, breasts, and belly. All the good food and protein shakes I'd been putting in front of her for the last week were already filling her out. God, I loved touching her.

Her hands wandered over my body. Her fingers brushed over an old bullet wound on my back. She slipped behind me and I felt the brush of her lips on my back.

Fuck, she undid me.

I tugged her back in front of me. Next, I poured some shampoo in my palm and worked it into her hair. I took my time massaging her scalp.

I loved taking care of her. For a long time, I'd believed being an assassin for my country was my calling.

I knew I'd been wrong. At the end, that work had taken too much from me. I'd gotten out before it had destroyed me. But here, looking after Georgie, I thought maybe I'd found my true calling.

To protect her, care for her, give her everything she deserved.

I washed the last of the suds away from her hair. She smiled up at me and I kissed her, slowly and deeply.

Then I lifted her again and carried her to bed.

"Nash, we're wet."

"I don't care." I laid her down on the covers. "I want you in my bed."

"I've been sleeping here for days."

I lowered my body to hers. "I want you in my bed, *with* me." I smiled. "I want you screaming my name again."

"I did not scream it."

"Did too."

She poked her tongue out at me.

She was already so much happier than she had been when I'd first found her in that dirty alley. I kissed her again. Then I let my lips drift across her nose, her cheek. "I love your freckles. Loved them when you were seventeen, love them now."

My mouth brushed her jaw. I bit her ear and she gasped.

"This time, I'm going slow," I murmured. "I'm taking my time."

She shivered, her hazel eyes glowing.

"I'm going to worship every inch of you. Then you'll fall asleep with me still inside you. Knowing nothing and no one will disturb your sleep."

"*Nash*." Her voice was filled with warmth, wonder.

I shifted, letting my mouth travel down her neck, to the swell of her breasts.

"If there's anything you don't like, tell me. If there's anything you want, just ask."

Her hand pressed to my cheek, a serious look on her pretty face. "Are you real? I keep thinking I'll wake up and have imagined you."

"I'm real, baby." I nipped at her nipple and she jerked. "And I'm all yours."

Then I sucked that nipple in my mouth and got to work on pleasuring her.

CHAPTER 30
GEORGIE

Today I ached for very different reasons than I had the week before.

I held onto Nash's hand as we headed to the Avernus security office. My leg muscles told me that I'd gotten a good workout last night, but not quite as much as the soreness between my thighs did. I also had a few faint bruises and bite marks.

I grinned. I'd never felt better.

Last night had been amazing.

Nash slung an arm around my shoulders. "I like that smile. What are you thinking about?"

My smile widened. "You. Last night."

He stopped, warmth filling his rugged face. Then he pulled me closer and kissed me.

It only took a second for me to get lost in it. Lost in the taste of him, the heat of him, the feel of him.

He pulled back and rubbed his nose against mine. "Get used to it. I've got more planned for later."

I shivered at the promise in his voice.

We entered the casino and took the elevator down to

the security office. Bastian, Cole, Alessio, and Landon were already in the conference room. My flush of pleasure faded as reality seeped back in.

The trip to the club last night—that I'd been trying my best *not* to think about—came back to the front of my mind. Snyder, and my driving need to take him down, were front and center.

I'm going to get him, Viv.

"Morning." Bastian nodded as we entered the conference room.

Nash closed the door behind us, his gaze going straight to the screens. They were all showing pictures of Snyder's mansion. It was sprawling and had vaguely Tuscan lines. Arched windows with black frames and a dark, tiled roof contrasted with the cream walls. Palm trees dotted the grounds along with immaculate landscaping.

I saw aerial photos showing a stage being set up behind the house, and what looked like bars with crates of empty glasses stacked beside them. An army of workers were setting things up by a huge pool and paved outdoor area. There were delivery trucks driving in and out of the front gates.

"The party is tomorrow night," Bastian said. "He's had deliveries going in and out all morning. There's going to be a massive fireworks display, dancing, all kinds of entertainment. This is it. The chance to take him down."

Tomorrow. My hands flexed then curled into fists. I felt Nash's gaze on me. I looked at him and nodded.

"There's a big guest list." Landon crossed his arms, frowning at the screens. "There'll be a lot of people."

"Sometimes it's best to hide in the crowd," Alessio murmured.

Cole nodded. "People don't remember things in a crowd. They're never focused on individuals."

"We do have one snag," Bastian said. "We can't hack Snyder's home CCTV. It's locked down tight. I'm guessing he has a discrete system that isn't connected to the internet."

"Dammit," Nash murmured. "I don't want to go in blind. We need to have eyes on him and his men."

"We could go in and plant some cameras," Cole suggested.

Nash nodded and glanced back at the screen. "If we do it right, we can smuggle some weapons in at the same time. That way there isn't a chance of us getting caught bringing them in for the party."

The men all nodded.

"And now's an excellent time to go in." Nash pointed to the screen where a white delivery van was driving through the black-iron gates. "I'll go in as a deliveryman."

"I have a batch of tiny surveillance cameras," Bastian said. "They're easy to plant, hard to detect, and they'll piggyback off his wi-fi." He smiled. "I also have a tiny hacker bug. If you plant it close to his router, we might just be able to hack his system from the inside."

I stepped forward. "I'm coming with you."

Nash's face hardened.

"This is *my* mission, Nash. I need to be a part of it."

His mouth flattened.

"I want to help plant the cameras. I'll stay with you, I won't do anything crazy, but I'm coming and I'm helping."

Beside Nash, Bastian smiled. "I'll pull some strings. Find a delivery due today that you can do. Going in as a couple will be good cover."

Nash shot him a narrow stare.

Bastian held out his hands. "I'm sure his security will be on the lookout for a lone woman. And a big, grumpy guy who clearly looks like he was in the military might get extra attention from the security guards."

Nash looked back at me, then sighed. "Fine."

I beamed up at him.

————

I bounced a little in the seat of the delivery van as Nash slowed. We were approaching the front gate to Snyder's mansion.

They were tall, made of black iron, and as ostentatious as the rest of his residence. The man wouldn't know class if it kicked him in the head.

I bounced again. The suspension in the van sucked.

We were both wearing navy coveralls and ball caps. Both had the logo for the Divine Elegance florist on them. Someone there had owed Bastian a favor.

I saw a security guard with a clipboard wave us to a stop.

Nerves winged through me, but I tried to look calm. Today, I wore a curly, blonde wig. The curls were escaping from under my cap. I also had some latex prosthetic stuff on my cheeks that Nash had given me. It changed the shape of my jawline.

He lowered the window. "Got a delivery of flowers. Divine Elegance florist."

The guard checked the clipboard. A second guard circled the truck, and I heard them open the back doors. I knew he'd be staring at the loads of flowers in giant urns packed into the back.

The tiny cameras I planned to plant were in my bra.

The cameras were so small. Bastian clearly liked his high-tech toys. The weapons Nash had brought were already tucked deep into the center of the flower arrangements.

Finally, the guard nodded. "Go around back. The flowers are all being set up by the pool."

With a nod, Nash drove on.

We were in.

I stared at the house and my throat tightened. Viv had lived here for a while.

While it was overblown for my tastes, it was grand. A modern palace. But for Viv, it had become a prison.

Nash parked. "Ready?"

I tugged on the bill of my cap and nodded.

We exited the van, and he opened the back. The enormous arrangements of colored flowers were in huge bronze urns. Nash hefted one out with ease and handed it to me. I struggled a little under the weight, but gritted my teeth and lugged it. He pulled a second one out. We followed a paved path through the neatly manicured and very green gardens. No xero-scaping for Snyder. His water bill had to be astronomical.

We rounded the house and then I saw the pool. My mouth dropped open.

It looked like a resort. The huge pool had sinuous curves and sparkled bright blue. There were cabanas on one side and a rock fountain with water falling into the pool at the far end.

There were people setting circular flower arrangements to float in the water. The entire pool was filled with flowers. I put my urn down.

"Holy cow," I murmured. "This place…"

Nash just grunted. He slipped a hand in the pocket of his coveralls and looked so casual as he planted a tiny camera on the pole of the cabana beside him. "Let's spread out. We'll plant most of our…items out here. Then we'll walk back through the house and plant a few inside."

We circled the pool. There was a large stage front and center, where DJ equipment was being set up. Several smaller stages were dotted around. The bars were all set up. I carefully planted a few cameras, trying to get good angles.

There were also some tall braziers spaced around. They'd be perfect for when the weather got colder once the sun had set.

Nash jerked his head at me and I followed him. We crossed onto a large terrace filled with circular tables and chairs. He pulled me inside through some giant sliding doors.

"What if we get caught?" I whispered.

"We'll just say we're taking a shortcut back to the truck."

We were in a massive living room. Everything was white. White carpet, white couch, some white statues.

I froze. Some of the pictures and videos of Viv that Snyder had taunted me with…they were taken in here.

She'd been hurt here.

My heart squeezed.

"Hey."

Nash touched my arm. I looked blindly at his worried face. "He hurt her here. They all did."

He took my hand and his fingers tangled with mine. "They won't hurt anybody else. Let's plant the last camera."

With a nod, I wandered past the couch and pressed it to the leg of a glossy table.

"Hey, what are you doing in here?"

My head jerked up and I saw a guard. *Damn.* It was Alden. My mouth went dry.

"Just heading back to our truck," Nash said, his tone unconcerned. "I thought an urn of flowers was going in here. We were just looking at the best way to bring it in."

Alden scowled. "No. All flowers are going outside by the pool."

Nash held his hands up. "Sorry, man. You're our sixth delivery for the day. Must've gotten it mixed up."

The guard relaxed and jerked his head. "Fine. Go and finish up."

Keeping my head down, I followed Nash out the front door. Back in the sunlight, I pulled in a deep breath. We'd done it.

I grinned up at Nash.

He smiled back. "Let's get out of here."

CHAPTER 31
NASH

I was dressed in black.

I was ready for Snyder's party. My black shirt was tucked into my black suit pants. I wanted this done. I never felt excitement or anticipation before a kill.

With Georgie involved, I just wanted this over.

I wanted her back here, safe and happy and unharmed.

"Snyder lost a lucrative real estate deal today," Bastian said smugly. "He won't care in a few hours, but he'll be smarting about it right now."

My friend looked very pleased with himself.

We were all standing beside the Range Rover, ready to go. Like me, the others were all dressed for the party and wearing dark colors. Landon wore a dark-blue shirt under his black suit, while Cole wore a black leather jacket. Allesio wore a black shirt tucked into dark-gray pants. I never saw the guy wear much color.

Bastian wore a black turtleneck with a three-quarter coat over the top. He looked like he was going to a damn fashion show.

We were all armed with hidden weapons. Small knives

and garrote wires were easy to conceal. What we couldn't easily hide and smuggle in were in the vases of flowers that Georgie and I had left behind.

Now, we just needed Georgie.

I glanced at my watch. The party had started. We planned to arrive after it was in full swing. Our arrival would be less noticeable, then.

I heard the door of my villa open and turned.

I almost swallowed my tongue.

Bastian gave a low laugh. "You should see your face."

"The man is *so* gone," Landon murmured.

I ignored them.

She walked toward us with a swing in her hips.

The jumpsuit was dark green and gleamed in the light. It sheathed her body like a glove. It had long pants, was nipped in at the waist, and there were tiny straps over her bare shoulders. In her hand, she held something black and fluffy that I guessed was a faux fur coat and not a dead Muppet.

She was wearing a black wig again, but this one was long and pulled up in a sleek ponytail.

"You look…" I had no words.

Her red lips curved. "Thanks."

The beaten, dejected woman was gone and she now shone with confidence and vitality. I knew she was focused on taking Snyder down tonight.

Tonight, she'd finally avenge her sister.

"Let's do this," she said.

I stepped forward and took her hand. We climbed into Bastian's SUV.

The drive to Summerlin was quiet. On one side of me, Georgie sat with her hands resting on her thighs. On the other, Cole was checking the knife he had hidden in his boot. Landon and Allesio were behind us.

"The cameras are up," Bastian said from the front seat. "I have Theo providing comms for us. Keep your phones close. I'll pass on anything relevant. Theo says the place is packed, and there are several guards doing rounds. Snyder is in prime form. Lording over the party like an emperor."

Sounded like Snyder.

Soon we reached the mansion and were directed to a parking spot by an attendant. There were lots of expensive vehicles lined up. Cole opened the door and slid out. I followed and heard music pumping. The house was lit up and strobe lights speared into the sky. I also noted several security guards strolling around.

Georgie looked a little nervous. She smoothed her hands down the front of her jumpsuit, then fluffed the cropped fur jacket she'd pulled on. I squeezed the back of her neck and she relaxed.

We entered the house, passing through the large front door flanked by giant potted plants. As we moved through the living area, following some other guests, I saw the back sliding doors were all thrown open.

People were packed around the pool, holding drinks. The braziers were on, and several women in tiny dresses were clustered around them to keep warm.

There was a DJ with headphones standing on a raised platform. There were already some guests dancing to the music and a few couples making out.

"Let's split up," I said. "Landon and Cole, you have Alden. Bastian and Alessio, you find Bruno. Georgie and I will look for Snyder."

My friends all nodded.

They dissolved into the crowd with practiced ease. I

kept an arm snug around Georgie as we wandered through the party and along the edge of the pool. The gauzy white curtains on the pool gazebos danced around in the breeze. Inside them, I could see people drinking and talking.

"Stay close." I nabbed a drink off a tray. I needed to look the part.

"Oh, look." Georgie pointed.

There were acrobats and performers on the grass. I watched a muscular man throw a tiny woman in a glittery leotard into the night sky. She landed on his palm and balanced, her arms in the air.

The crowd around them clapped.

Nearby, a man and a woman in red outfits were spinning burning sticks. They whirled them fast and it looked like a wheel of flames. The crowd oohed and ahhed.

"No expense spared," Georgie murmured. "Viv was so awed by his parties. At first. She was so sure he'd help her achieve her dreams."

I pulled her close and pressed a kiss to the top of her head. I knew she still hadn't properly grieved for her sister.

She would. After she had her revenge. After this was over.

We continued on. Snyder wouldn't be far away.

The phone in my pocket vibrated. I pulled it out and saw a text from Bastian.

Snyder on the north side of the pool. Near the cabanas.

I guided Georgie that way. We passed more entertainers—two couples who were dancing. They were doing some Latin dances, the men tossing the women around like they weighed nothing. Nearby, partygoers watched and clapped.

Then Georgie stiffened.

I followed her gaze and saw Snyder.

Yeah, the bastard was holding court. He had both arms around two young women. They were smiling up at him, hanging on his every word. He was talking with a small group of people. He was nodding, and occasionally touching the women. A stroke of a hip, a squeeze of an arm, a brush against their cheek.

Then I felt Georgie look to the left. I spotted Shandy. The singer wore a floaty, silver-gray dress. She was watching Snyder with the women, hurt and confusion on her face.

When Snyder let one of the women pepper kisses along his jaw, Shandy looked away, clearly upset.

I squeezed Georgie's arm. "After tonight, she'll be free."

She bobbed her head. "Soon, it will all be over."

There was a finality in her voice that made my gut clench.

Yes, Snyder would be over, but not us.

Maybe Georgie didn't realize it yet, but she was mine. I'd warned her when she hadn't left that there would be consequences.

I was never letting her go.

CHAPTER 32
GEORGIE

Nash and I walked to the urn of flowers beside the pool. I looked at the water. The beautiful flower arrangements were floating serenely on the surface.

The beauty masked the rot of this place.

Nash checked his phone and leaned closer. "Landon and Cole followed Alden. He's gone out alone for a cigarette."

I licked my lips. I knew that Alden wouldn't be returning to the party. This unsettled me, but I wasn't sorry. I remembered Viv, I remember the other women.

Nash cupped my cheek. His callused fingers whispered over my skin.

"Okay?"

I nodded. Once again, he was taking care of me.

I loved him touching me. I loved him being by my side.

My insides trembled.

I loved him.

I realized that I'd always loved him. First, as a young

handsome boy who'd been my brother's best friend, and now as a tough, hard, dangerous man.

I'd fought not to fall, but I'd been defenseless against him.

God. He lowered his head, his mouth brushing mine. I pushed into the kiss, opening my lips to his.

Then I realized at the same time, he was reaching into the flowers. Quickly, he pulled the guns out. They both had silencers attached. I slid one under my fur coat, then into the sparkly crossbody bag I wore.

His disappeared under his jacket. I looked up at him.

Then I caught a glimpse of a familiar man over his shoulder.

"Bruno," I hissed.

Calmly, Nash curled his arm around me and turned us. While it looked like he was just studying the party, I knew he was taking in Bruno.

Snyder's right-hand man was with a woman in a red dress. She had a mass of black curls that fell down the middle of her back and was tottering on four-inch heels. He was holding her close, gesturing around, like he was giving her a tour.

The couple disappeared into the house.

Rage welled. I remembered the emotionless way he'd beaten me. I remembered the things he'd done to my sister.

He loved his role as Snyder's enforcer. He enjoyed beating up competitors, abusing women, killing rivals.

"Come on." Nash took my hand and we headed through the crowd. We sidestepped to avoid a drunken trio pouring champagne. The golden liquid overflowed their glasses, spilling onto the ground.

Inside the house was warmer and quieter. I took a few

calming breaths. I couldn't see Bruno and the woman anywhere. Nash and I walked through the living area. They couldn't have gone far.

Then I spotted movement. The couple appeared from a hallway, Bruno waving at some art on the wall.

Nash grabbed me and pulled me in for a kiss. He ran his hands down my body, and getting into the moment, I slid my hands in his hair. I giggled for effect.

Out of the corner of my eye, I noted that Bruno barely gave us more than a passing glance.

"Let me show you upstairs, beautiful." He pressed a beefy hand to the woman's lower back and led her up the curving staircase.

"They're gone," I whispered against Nash's mouth.

He nipped my lips. "We need to separate him from her, then take him down."

I felt electric. My hands flexed. This was happening.

We walked quietly up the stairs. At the top was a long, wide hallway with a plush carpet. It was empty.

Where did they go? Then I heard a muffled noise from a nearby room. It was followed by a woman's sharp cry.

Oh, God. She sounded like she was in distress.

Nash and I burst forward. I tested the handle and found the door locked. Behind it, I heard the woman cry out again.

"No! Stop. Let me go."

Nash lifted his boot and kicked the door in.

Bruno had the struggling woman pinned to the bed. She was on her belly, her dress rucked up around her waist, and he had a knee pressed to her back. He was working to unfasten his belt. One strap of the woman's dress was torn, her breast hanging out. She had a slap mark on her cheek.

"Help me!" she cried, tears pouring down her face.

Bruno scowled at us. "Get out."

I reached into my bag and pulled out the gun. I aimed directly at his chest. "Let her go."

Bruno hesitated.

I met his gaze. "Do it."

Whatever he saw convinced him. He took his knee off the woman.

She scrambled up, covering her bare breast. She staggered off the bed with a sob, then almost tripped as she ran out the door.

Nash closed it behind her, although the lock was broken from his kick.

"Who the fuck are you?" Bruno turned to face us, his gaze on Nash.

"It's not me you need to worry about," Nash drawled.

Bruno's brow creased, then his gaze flicked back to me.

"You won't hurt any more women," I said. "You won't rape them, you won't beat them, and you won't kill them."

His eyes widened a little. "Viv's sister?" He laughed. "Man, you don't give up and you don't learn. I see you brought backup this time. Won't be enough."

"*I'm* enough," I said.

Without any warning, he lunged at me.

Nash intercepted him. With one punch to the face, followed by a chop to the throat, Bruno dropped to the floor with a pained sound.

He clutched his neck, wincing. "Fucking asshole." He swiped at the blood on his face.

"Not so easy when you aren't attacking someone half your size," Nash growled.

I held the gun aimed on Bruno. It felt heavy in my hand, especially with the silencer attached. He'd been about to rape that woman. He had zero remorse. He didn't care.

"Viv was an addict and a whore," Bruno said. "Just like the rest of them. She might have whined and cried, but she loved cock. She loved me choking her while I fucked her." His smile turned ugly. "Maybe I'll take your guy down, then make him watch while I fuck you the same way—"

I pulled the trigger.

The muffled shot was still loud. It hit him in the neck and blood spurted.

With a sharp cry, he clamped a hand over it.

"You don't get to hurt anyone anymore. This ends now. You end here."

Bruno slumped, choking on blood.

The next bullet I put between his eyes.

He fell to the carpet.

I'd done it.

I'd killed him.

"That's for Viv," I whispered. "And for me."

A warm hand curled around my shoulder. "You did well, sweetheart."

I pushed back into Nash's strength. I was shaking a little, but with him beside me, I felt safe.

He squeezed again, then stepped forward. He crouched and wrapped Bruno in the rug on the floor. Then I watched as he dragged Bruno's body to the walk-in closet and shoved him inside.

Nash pulled out his phone and texted. "I'll have Theo scrub the internal cameras. They'll be no images of us in the house."

I swallowed. Part of this was over. I couldn't believe it.

Bruno had haunted my nightmares. I'd relived every second of both his beatings.

He was gone, but we still had Snyder to deal with.

"What about the bullets?" I asked.

"They're untraceable. The gun has no serial number, no history." He touched my cheek. "One down."

"One to go."

A beeping came from the closet and Nash frowned. He opened the door, crouched, and quickly rummaged in Bruno's pockets. He pulled out a cellphone.

I saw a flashing red message on the screen.

Security alert.

Nash scanned it and cursed.

"What is it?" I asked.

His face was grim. "Bruno got a warning off to Snyder. He knows we're coming."

CHAPTER 33
NASH

UNSANCTIONED
SERIES

W e hurried down the stairs. Once we got outside, Georgie ditched her fur coat on a chair on the terrace. Her gun was tucked back in her bag.

I pressed the phone to my ear, and a second later Bastian answered.

"Bruno's been eliminated," I clipped. "He got a warning off to Snyder."

Bastian cursed.

Georgie and I moved into the crowd of partygoers. The music was louder and more people were dancing.

"Where's Snyder?"

"He was in a pool cabana, cavorting with three women," Bastian replied.

My lip curled. I kept Georgie close as we moved toward the pool. The cabanas were on the other side to us.

A second later, there was a giant *boom*. Georgie jerked beside me. Fireworks filled the sky overhead.

Everyone looked up, the crowd oohing. Multicolored

sparks filled the night sky. More booms followed, more explosions of light.

I didn't watch the fireworks. I scanned the pool and saw someone else wasn't watching the display either. Snyder was hurrying out of one of the cabanas, his phone clutched in his hand.

Georgie and I watched him. He must have sensed us because he stopped and lifted his head. His gaze locked on us.

Then he turned and was swallowed up by the throng of people.

"Bastian, he's on the move."

"Wait, I'll get Theo to access the cameras." There was a pause. "Got him. Theo says Snyder is heading to the far end of the house. He slipped into a side door."

I tugged Georgie along the pool. The crowd *ahhed* as the fireworks continued and no one paid any attention to us. We moved along the outside of the house and ahead, I spotted a door ajar.

Inside, we found ourselves in a wine cellar. The large space was filled with backlit, built-in shelving filled with dozens and dozens of bottles of wine. I heard the sound of a door closing and spun.

"Stay behind me," I warned Georgie.

We moved down a short hall, then I yanked open a door.

We stepped into a well-equipped gym. There were weight racks, exercise machines, and mirrors on the walls.

And Snyder sprinting through it.

"Snyder!" Georgie yelled.

He looked back, then pulled a gun from under his jacket. He fired.

I leaped at Georgie and took her to the rubber floor

behind a weight bench. More bullets hit the wall above us and she cried out. I moved my body over hers, shielding her.

The shooting stopped. I waited a beat, then lifted my head. Through the machines I saw that Snyder was gone.

"We can't lose him," she said.

I pulled her up. I pulled my gun out and she did the same. We crossed the gym and reached the door Snyder had escaped through.

We paused on either side of it. She nodded, then I cracked it open.

I could see cars. It was a garage.

Staying crouched, we slid inside. It was the biggest garage I'd ever seen. We cautiously moved inside, looking for our target. I pressed a finger to my lips and Georgie nodded.

The place was fancy as hell. The floors were polished concrete and the walls were painted black. Lines of modern LED lights ran along the ceiling, illuminating the row of expensive cars. I saw a Ferrari, a Lamborghini, an Aston Martin DBX SUV, a McLaren, and more.

There was no sound. No sign of him.

Where did he go?

I pointed, and Georgie and I moved past the Ferrari, using it for cover. She was staying right behind me.

Come on, Snyder.

I heard a squeak of a shoe on the polished concrete and spun.

A russet-haired security guard leaped at us from behind a Mercedes SUV.

Georgie cried out. He rammed her into the next car, then kicked at me.

My SIG went flying and skidded under another car.

Fuck. I lunged at the guy.

My first punch hit his gut, the second his chest. He fell back with a yowl.

But he wasn't a quitter.

He lowered a shoulder and charged at me.

He hit me hard, and my body slammed into a car behind me. Pain radiated up my back but I ignored it. When he swung at my face, I ducked, then landed a double punch into his gut, and shoved him off me.

We spun, and I sent his body flying against another car. A car alarm started blaring.

I wrapped my arms around his neck and got him in a headlock. I pulled back, cutting off his air. He choked, grabbing desperately at my arm.

Gritting my teeth, I held on.

Georgie was watching. Her gaze was steady, no fear or panic on her face. She watched as I choked the guy into unconsciousness. He sagged and I dropped him.

"We have to find Snyder," she said.

I scanned the cars. "He's here."

My gun was gone, but I knelt down and grabbed the guard's. I checked it, and then we moved down the line of vehicles.

I was proud of Georgie. She was focused, determined, brave. So damn brave.

I loved her.

Damn, of course I loved her. I'd loved her since she was a teenager. Every fierce, sweet, and vulnerable inch of her.

I'd spend the rest of my life loving her, working to deserve her.

I heard a noise and we both swiveled. Something was rolling on the floor. Crouching, I took a step closer.

Georgie turned, her eyes widening. She was looking in the opposite direction to the noise.

"Nash!"

I sensed someone behind me...a second too late.

Something hard slammed into my head.

Pain cut through me like a shockwave.

My vision turned to black splotches and I staggered. I couldn't go down. I couldn't leave Georgie alone and undefended.

Another blow cracked into my skull.

I crashed to the concrete and heard Georgie scream. My nerveless fingers dropped the gun. My legs wouldn't move, my arms wouldn't move. Pain throbbed through my head.

I saw Georgie's pretty shoes.

Fight it, Oakley.

She needs you.

But I couldn't move. The pain was too much. It had claws and it latched onto me, digging in deep, and dragging me under.

CHAPTER 34
GEORGIE

I n horror, I watched Nash fall to the floor.

My insides froze and all my muscles locked. I couldn't breathe.

Nash.

He'd gone down hard. Snyder stood over him, clutching a tire iron. He reared his arm back, about to hit Nash again.

"No!" I lunged forward and knocked his arm away.

The tire iron flew through the air and hit the windshield of a sportscar. The glass cracked.

Snyder shoved into me. I fell on my ass.

My gaze locked on Nash. He wasn't moving. I saw blood on his head.

Help him, Georgie. Protect him.

Nausea welled. How badly was he hurt? I couldn't lose him.

I scrambled to my feet and pulled out my handgun. I aimed at Snyder.

At the man who'd caused me so much pain. Who'd caused much death and destruction.

The man who'd hurt the ones I loved.

He'd killed Viv.

He'd hurt Nash.

I swallowed and stared at Snyder.

He made a scoffing sound, scorn on his handsome face. "You haven't got what it takes to kill me." He pulled out his own gun.

He didn't aim at me.

He aimed down at Nash.

"Now, me, I'm happy to pull the trigger. I'll fill your hired muscle with bullets, then you're next."

I felt sick. I wanted to shoot him.

For my sister.

I wanted him dead.

But if I fired, he could get a shot off and kill Nash.

Emotions tangled in a knot around my throat.

I'm sorry, Viv. I can't lose him.

I couldn't let Snyder kill Nash.

I loved him.

I wanted to live. I wanted to be with Nash.

Love was scary, a risk. There was always a chance of loss, but it didn't take away from the fact that love was worth every second.

I'm sorry I can't get you justice, Viv.

I lowered the gun.

Snyder smirked at me and stepped over Nash. He came at me fast.

Shoving me against the car, he pressed his forearm against my throat. He pinned me there, cutting off my air. He lifted his gun and jammed the barrel against my temple. His face was an inch from mine.

"I *always* win. I always get what I want."

My mouth flattened. I vowed that I would take him down.

But for now, I needed Nash safe.

My need for revenge was not worth his life.

Snyder pushed harder. I choked and grabbed at his arm. He smiled, enjoying my pain and panic.

Then he pulled back.

I coughed and rubbed my neck. That's when I heard shouts.

We both turned. Men were entering the garage and my heart leaped. I recognized Bastian, Landon, and the others.

Snyder cursed.

More shouts, and I spotted several guards running through the cars, coming from the other direction. Gunfire filled the garage, echoing loudly.

"Dammit." Snyder grabbed my arm and dragged me away from the fighting.

"Let me go." I tried to jerk free.

"Oh no. I'm not having you pop up again and try to kill me."

He stopped beside a low-slung, blue Lamborghini.

He opened the passenger door and shoved me inside. "Don't move, or I'll shoot the guy." He slammed the door closed.

I pressed my hands to my knees, my fingers digging into my skin. Through the window, I saw Nash's body on the floor.

He was so still.

Please be okay. Please.

Snyder slid into the driver's seat. He started the engine and it roared to life.

He tapped something on the dash, and ahead of us, the

large garage door started opening. I looked back at Nash. Beyond him, I saw people running our way.

Bastian and the others would help him. He'd be okay.

Snyder slammed his foot down on the gas. We tore out of the garage, the vehicle fishtailing as we hit the driveway. I scrambled to fasten my seatbelt. He sped down the driveway and out through the front gates.

He turned left.

"Where are we going?"

"Just shut up."

CHAPTER 35
NASH

"**N**ash? Nash? Wake the hell up."

Bastian's annoying voice buzzed in my ear. I groaned.

I felt hands probing up my head and it hurt like hell.

I tried to slap them away and opened my eyes.

Everything was blurry for a second, then coalesced into Landon staring down at me, his face serious. The others stood behind him.

I groaned again, my head throbbing.

"He's okay," Landon said. "Possible concussion."

I sat up and my skull tried to leap sideways off my neck. I grabbed my forehead with one hand. "I don't have a concussion."

Landon sighed. "Just because you say it, doesn't make it true. How's your vision?"

"Fine." Things were still a little blurry, but I could see. I didn't mention the monster headache I had brewing.

I blinked. That's when our location came into focus.

We were in a garage. I saw expensive cars.

Snyder.

I stiffened. "Georgie. Where's Georgie?" I glanced around.

"She's alive," Cole said, face grim.

"Where?" I staggered to my feet, and Cole grabbed my arm to help me up.

"Snyder shoved her in a lambo and sped off," Bastian said.

My chest locked. Fuck. *Fuck.* "He's got her?"

"Only until we get her back," Bastian said.

I looked around, trying to think through the rush of fear. The garage door was open and outside, I heard the dull pops of fireworks.

I had to get to Georgie.

The nearest car was a gray McLaren GTS. That would do. I marched toward it.

"You're *not* driving." Bastain cut me off. "Not after the blow to the head you just took. Besides, I'm a better driver."

"You are not."

"Fine, I'm a faster driver."

I couldn't argue with that. Besides, we were wasting time. I yanked open the door and got in the passenger seat. Beside us, I saw Landon, Cole, and Alessio getting into the DBX SUV.

Bastian started the engine, revving it. It had a throaty, powerful growl. A second later, he sped out of the garage.

The gate at the end of the driveway was open, but the guards were waving at us. We raced past them. The DBX was right behind us.

Bastian pulled out on the road and touched the dash. "Theo? You there?"

"I'm here." The head of security's deep voice filled the car.

"We need the location of Snyder's Lamborghini. He pulled out of his place a few minutes ahead of us."

"Hold on. Snyder has LoJack on all his cars." There was a pause that was probably only seconds, but felt like hours. "Got him. He's heading out of Vegas. Into the desert."

"We need to catch him," I said.

Bastian nodded, his lips curling. "Your wish is my command."

He sped up, and I pressed a hand to the roof. Bastian hadn't lied. He drove fast.

Hold on, Georgie. Hold on for me.

It felt like there was a rock in my chest. What if Snyder hurt her? Shot her?

"Here." Bastian held out a handgun.

I took the Glock and drew in a steadying breath. "I can't lose her, Bastian."

"I know. You won't." He turned the wheel, overtaking a slower car.

"She's...everything to me. I always knew it, but I fought it. I thought it was better to leave her alone. She makes me smile, makes me want to take care of her, to make her happy. She makes me a better man."

My friend met my gaze. "You deserve that. We're getting her back."

"Take the next turn onto the highway," Theo said. "He's just a few miles ahead of you."

Bastian accelerated. Landon and the others had fallen back a little, but they weren't too far behind.

The highway had emptied out. Empty desert whizzed past on either side of us. Only a few minutes later, I saw red taillights ahead of us. My heart leaped.

I'm right here, sweetheart.

Snyder wouldn't leave this desert alive.

He'd touched my woman, taken her, hurt her.

Now, I'd hurt him.

Bastian closed the distance to the Lamborghini. The road was still empty, and a second later, he pulled out into the other lane and roared up alongside the other car.

I stared out the side window, and Snyder glanced my way. His face was tight. I looked past him and saw Georgie. Her face was pale, her eyes locked on me.

I lowered the window.

I couldn't shoot at Snyder. I couldn't risk hitting her.

Instead, I raised the gun and aimed at the front of the Lamborghini.

Bullets pinged on metal.

Snyder jerked the wheel and the Lamborghini veered. Our cars almost collided.

Cursing, Bastian reacted with lightning quick reflexes. He pulled back a little, and Snyder sped forward.

"Get alongside him again," I ordered. "Get us close. And hold us steady." I unbuckled my seat belt.

Bastian uttered a curse. "Oh no. This is a dumb idea. You know jumping onto a moving car is way harder than it looks in the movies."

"And yet, we've both done it before."

"You'll kill yourself."

"I'm *not* leaving her with that asshole. He could shoot her. He could crash. No, this ends now."

"*Fuck.*" Bastian's hands gripped the wheel, a muscle ticking in his jaw. Then he hit the gas.

We pulled up beside the Lamborghini again. Inside the

car, I saw Georgie yanking on Snyder's arm. Snyder's mouth was moving, cursing, no doubt.

I tucked the handgun in the waistband of my pants. Then I climbed out through the side window.

Bastian moved us closer, only inches between the two speeding cars.

I jumped.

CHAPTER 36
GEORGIE

h God.

Snyder was speeding so fast. Nash and Bastian were beside us. Thankfully the road was empty.

For now.

My heart was pumping hard. One wrong move and Snyder could kill us all.

As I watched, Nash climbed out of the window, clinging to the top of the sports car.

I couldn't breathe. Surely, he wasn't going to jump?

"Stop!" I yelled at Snyder. "Stop the car."

"Fuck, no!" He elbowed me away.

"It's over, Snyder. I won't stop coming after you. *Ever.* You killed my sister. You've hurt so many people. I won't let you get away with that."

"I always get away with it," he yelled. "I do whatever the hell I want. No one's going to stop me."

"Not this time." I grabbed his arm. "That man out there, he won't let you live. He'll never stop helping me.

He's the opposite of you. A good, honorable, supportive man."

Snyder scoffed.

The other car came closer, Nash clinging to the side.

My heart leaped into my throat. *Oh God, no.*

He jumped.

I heard a thump and Snyder cursed.

Nash was partly on top of the roof, partly hanging onto the windshield. Then he shifted. I saw him through the glass, the wind tearing at his clothes and hair.

He looked like a dark knight.

My dark knight.

I smiled at him.

Then Snyder wrenched the wheel to the side.

I screamed and was tossed against the door. I saw Nash jerk, his body thrown sideways.

No. *No.*

If he fell at this speed, he'd die for sure.

"*Stop.*" I smacked at Snyder. Not just for Viv, but for Nash and me as well. I whacked at the man's head.

Outside, Nash regained balance. He met my gaze through the windshield.

I was so in love with this man. This brave man who'd proven to me that he'd take care of me, that he'd kill for me. That he'd stand by my side and give me everything I needed.

Nash raised a gun. He aimed it directly at Snyder.

Snyder snarled.

Nash fired. The bullet hit the glass. It didn't penetrate, but a spider web of cracks appeared.

Snyder slammed on the brakes and I gasped, flying forward. The seatbelt dug into my chest. But Nash had anticipated the move. He threw himself against the car, holding on hard.

We slowed down, tires squealing.

Then I heard a honking horn. My head whipped up and ahead I saw car headlights piercing the night.

Beside us, Bastian dropped back, sliding in behind our car.

The oncoming car whizzed past us, still honking.

Nash aimed the gun again. Snyder let out a frustrated noise and slammed his foot on the accelerator.

Nash fired.

The windscreen shattered and Snyder cried out.

Then suddenly, the car veered off the road.

No. We hit bumpy ground and I jerked against the seatbelt.

Where was Nash?

Then, the car flipped.

I screamed. Everything became a terrifying whirl.

We hit the sandy ground. I heard the crunch of metal and the sound of glass breaking. My head hit the side window, pain exploding through my skull.

I didn't know if I was up or down.

Where was Nash?

It was my last thought before everything went black.

CHAPTER 37
NASH

As soon as the Lamborghini hit the dirt, I jumped.

I didn't want to leave Georgie, but getting thrown or crushed by the car would kill me. I hoped like hell that it had slowed down enough that I wouldn't break every bone in my body.

But I was more worried about Georgie.

Be okay, sweetheart.

I hit the sandy dirt and rolled several times. The impact jarred every cell in my body. My already aching head throbbed harder. I came to a stop face down, the air knocked out of me. Sand sprayed my face and hair.

I stayed there for a second, a little stunned, dragging in air. I tried to clear my head.

I heard the crunch and squeal of metal.

Georgie.

I pushed onto my hands and knees. The entire world tried to climb sideways and I grabbed my head.

I heard the roar of an engine. I looked up.

The McLaren and the Aston Martin both screeched to a halt on the side of the highway. I saw dark silhouettes heading my way, and beams of cellphone flashlights cutting through the night.

Georgie. I turned my head and my insides squeezed to a tiny point.

Fuck.

The Lamborghini was a crushed, twisted mess, resting on its roof.

"No. *No*." I struggled to my feet and ran toward it.

Bastian and the others caught up with me.

"Take it easy, Nash." Landon gripped my arm.

"Fuck that." I yanked free. "Georgie! Georgie!"

I raced to the passenger side of the car. Damn, it was just crumpled metal. My heart felt like a block of stone. If I lost her…

I dropped to my knees.

And saw her. She was hanging upside down, held in place by the seatbelt. There was blood on her face and she wasn't moving.

"Georgie," I whispered.

Bastian shone his phone flashlight inside the car.

Then she turned her head and opened her beautiful eyes. "Nash?"

My heart flared to life. "I'm here, sweetheart. I'm going to get you out." I looked back over my shoulder. "I need a knife."

A blade was slapped into my palm. It was black, with a beautiful carved hilt. I knew it was one of Landon's.

Then I heard a moan from the driver's seat.

My jaw tightened. Snyder wasn't dead, but he wasn't my concern right now.

My priority was getting Georgie out.

"Hurry, Nash," Alessio said. "The gas tank was ruptured."

I smelled it now. The acrid scent of gas in the air. I reached in through the broken window and started sawing through the seatbelt. I wanted her out of the damn wreck.

Thank fuck Landon kept his knives lethally sharp.

The blade broke through the belt, and Georgie dropped down with a small cry.

"I've got you, baby. Hold on." I handed the knife back to Landon and reached inside for her. The door was bent and space was limited. I grabbed her and pulled. Her fingers gripped my arms as I hauled her out of the car.

"Nash."

I yanked her into my arms. I pressed her face to my chest and rocked. She clung to me.

She was alive. She was in my arms.

I realized now how truly afraid I'd been the moment I knew Snyder had her.

Her shaking hands cupped my cheeks. She had a small cut on her temple that was bleeding down the side of her face, but otherwise she looked fine.

She shifted, then pressed her mouth to mine.

I cupped the back of her head. I didn't kiss her, I devoured her.

"I was so scared when you jumped on the car," she murmured against my lips.

"I wasn't letting him hurt you."

She smiled. "I knew you'd come for me."

"I will *always* come for you."

A low, pained groan came from the car.

Georgie's head whipped around, her face changing.

She wriggled, trying to stand. Then Bastian was there, helping her up. I rose and dusted myself off.

Georgie stomped around the car.

It was worse on the other side, the metal ripped and twisted. The scent of gasoline was stronger too.

Snyder was caught in the twisted metal. There was blood on his face and his chest looked crushed.

"Get me…out," he croaked.

Georgie heaved in a breath. "You're exactly where you deserve to be." Then she reached over, and gripped the hilt of my gun resting in my waistband. She yanked it out.

Hand steady, she raised it and aimed at Snyder.

"No." Snyder's eyes went wide. "You can't—"

The single shot echoed through the night. Snyder slumped forward, no longer moving.

She handed the gun back to me.

"It's finally done." She raised her gaze to the night sky. "It's done, Viv. Like I promised. For you."

I slid an arm around her and looked at the others.

Bastian nodded. "Let's get out of here."

I had one more thing to do.

"Anyone got a lighter?" I asked.

"I do." Alessio slid a hand in his pocket, then handed it to me.

As we started to walk away, I ignited it with a click. Georgie glanced at the flickering flame, then at me. She nodded.

I tossed it behind us.

It hit the leaking gasoline and the flames rippled to life, engulfing the Lamborghini.

I kissed the top of her head. "Let's go home."

I hadn't burned the entire world down for her, just Snyder's world.

And I'd do it again in a heartbeat, for her.

CHAPTER 38
GEORGIE

I n the shower, I tilted my face to the spray.

I washed it all away. The blood, the dirt, the fear, the anger.

The grief would never leave. I'd always miss Viv, and Elliott, and my parents. But I didn't want it gone. Grief was just proof of how much I loved them.

Shutting off the water, I stepped out and felt lighter.

I was free.

In the mirror, I stared at my reflection. I saw a woman with a small cut on her temple, which thankfully wasn't too bad.

A woman who was no longer tired, alone, or running on fear and anger.

Just a woman. With possibilities ahead of her and who was in love with a sexy, strong man.

The bathroom door opened and through the mist from the shower, I saw him. He'd clearly showered in the guest room. His hair was damp and he was wearing black pajama pants that sat low on his narrow hips and no shirt.

He held up an ice pack. "I thought you might need this?"

"No, I'm fine."

"How's the cut?" He reached up and touched it, gently probing.

"Minor. How's your head?"

"Still attached."

Landon had checked him over when we'd returned to the Avernus. He'd given Nash the all clear, but told me to keep an eye on him. It was going to take me a long time to get the image of Snyder hitting Nash with a tire iron out of my head.

Snyder. I let the thought of him float away. He had no power over my life anymore.

Nash cocked his head. "You okay?"

I smiled "I am. I really am."

"It's been a hell of a night. I want you to lie down and rest." He was still holding the ice pack like he was trying to find a spot on my body that needed it.

I fought back a smile. My big, protective assassin. I closed the distance between us and pressed my hands to his chest.

Things shifted inside me, a growing need that had everything to do with him. Everything to do with love and desire. I pressed my lips to his chest and nipped.

"Georgie..."

I ran my mouth up his neck. God, I loved the taste of him. I went up on my toes and pressed my mouth to his.

With a groan, he gripped my jaw and kissed me back.

"The last thing I want to do is rest," I whispered.

His hands clamped on my hips. "Like I said, it was a hell of a night. You were abducted, you fought with Snyder, you killed him. It's a lot to take in."

"No. Tonight, Snyder no longer exists." I nipped his jaw. "What exists is us."

I kissed him again, before I slowly lowered to my knees in front of him.

"Georgie…" His voice deepened.

"I want you. I want you in my mouth." I rubbed my cheek against the hard bulge in his pants.

He made a low sound, his fingers sliding into my hair. "Then suck me, sweetheart. I need you to suck my cock, Georgie."

I pushed the waistband of his pants down and freed his cock. I licked my lips and circled his girth with my hand. Leaning forward, I took him in my mouth.

He groaned my name. I pressed my other hand to his strong thigh, sucking him deep. Right now, I didn't have it in me to take my time or tease him. I dragged my mouth up, swirled my tongue around the head, then lowered my head again.

"Christ, Georgie, your mouth…" His hips rocked forward.

I looked up, our gazes meshing. I sucked him harder, so my cheeks hollowed.

With a growl, he slid his hands under my armpits and hauled me up. Then he carried me across the bathroom in two long strides. My bare butt hit the cool marble of the vanity, and Nash shoved my legs wide. His hands clamped over my breasts, squeezing, thumbs flicking over my nipples.

I arched into him. I could no longer think. I was pure sensation.

"I need you inside me," I panted.

He made a low sound, and pushed my thighs wider with his hips. "Watch."

One of his hands circled his hard cock, and heat licked my insides. I couldn't look away as he lined up the thick head between my legs. Then he shoved forward.

I cried out. I was filled with Nash.

Filled with everything I needed.

With him, I wasn't alone. With him, I was loved.

Then he started to move. It was hard and fast, and my cries filled the bathroom. His hands slid under my ass and lifted me. He swiveled, and I found myself on my hands and knees on the bathroom mat.

He was behind me, thighs pressing against my ass. Then he was back inside me. He hammered into me hard. I threw my head back against his shoulder. His hand delved beneath my straining body and strummed my clit.

"*Nash.*" I came hard, pleasure washing over me in intense waves. My head spun and for a second, I worried that I'd pass out from the intensity.

He gripped my hips, and I knew I'd have bruises. He slammed into me one more time, and with a low roar, he poured himself inside me.

We were both panting. I wasn't sure I could move, but I didn't need to worry. Nash lifted me off the floor and carried me out of the bathroom.

He set me down on the bed, then climbed on and hauled me close.

I snuggled into him and sighed happily.

"You sure you don't need the ice pack?"

I laughed. "Absolutely. I'm good, Nash. Really good." I tilted my head back. "Thank you. For everything. For helping me, for caring for me. But most of all, for helping me take down Snyder. It was what I needed."

He stroked a hand through my hair. "You never need to thank me."

I breathed him in, listening to the steady thump of his heart. An uncomfortable niggle wormed through me.

My mission was done. Snyder had been my focus, but now he was dead.

Now, I needed to sort out my life.

Nash hadn't mentioned what happened next, but I couldn't just stay at his place. I wouldn't take advantage of him.

"I guess tomorrow I need to work out where I go next."

He stiffened. "Go?"

I nodded. "I need to think about a job, and about finding a place to live."

He stiffened even more.

I frowned. "Nash—"

"You live here." His voice was a growl. He rolled and pinned me under him. "You aren't leaving."

He was using his bossy tone.

"Nash, I can't just stay here. You've already done so much for me."

His rugged face hardened. "You *will* stay here. You're mine. I'm yours."

My belly tightened. "I—"

"I'm *not* letting you go, Georgie. I tried it once. It was the wrong decision."

My heart was giving tiny little flutters. "Why? Why do you want me to stay?"

A muscle in his jaw flexed. "Because we're good together."

"I need more than that," I whispered.

That muscle ticked again. "You're staying because I love you. I thought a different life would be better for you, but I was wrong. The best thing for you is me. A man who'll love you, protect you, always."

He loved me. My insides melted to goo. "You love me?"

"How can you not know?"

"I love you too, Nash. So much."

He made a noise, then his mouth was on mine, tongue finding mine. The kiss was deep and possessive.

"You're not leaving. Ever. I never want to hear you talk about leaving again."

I stroked his stubbled jaw. "I didn't mean that I was leaving you. I thought I'd find a rental apartment here in Las Vegas, and get a job—"

"You can find a job, or not. Whatever you want. But your home is here now. With me."

Tears welled in my eyes.

"Don't cry, sweetheart."

"They're happy tears."

"I don't care. No crying."

I fought back a smile. "I had nothing without you." My voice was thick. "Now, I have everything."

"And I'll make sure you always feel that way."

CHAPTER 39
NASH

"Okay, I want reports on the camera upgrades on my desk tomorrow." I flicked through the security file on my desk, then looked at Theo. "And the new training schedule needs a few tweaks. I emailed them to you."

The older man nodded. "Got it. It was a good session with the new guards today. They learned a lot from the training."

"Good." I glanced at my watch. "I'm heading out."

A smile flickered on Theo's craggy face. "You've been ready to leave for the last hour. Used to be, you'd sit here until late. But I guess having a beautiful woman waiting for you changes things."

I clapped his shoulder. "It sure does. See you tomorrow, Theo."

I headed out, eager to get back to the villa. Georgie was cooking dinner. Christmas was only a few days away and she'd declared that she was cooking Christmas lunch for me and the guys. She'd been testing out different recipes. I liked seeing her so excited.

It had been one week since we'd eliminated Snyder. I'd been keeping a careful eye on Georgie, waiting for any suppressed emotions or backlash or guilt to hit.

But she was fine. She was more than fine, she was happy.

Smiling, I stepped out of the elevator, then hurried outside to the path to the villas. A light rain was falling.

In addition to spending the week experimenting in the kitchen, she'd also been making candles with holiday scents. She'd made ones that smelled like gingerbread, another that smelled like eggnog, and another one that smelled like fir and spruce trees.

She'd told me that she had some things in storage and we'd had them shipped. We put a few pieces of her furniture in the villa, and the rest she'd donated. I'd helped her haul stuff to a charity that helped recovering addicts find their feet.

In addition to all of that, she'd also been busy looking at job ads. I'd told her not to rush it, but I could tell that she wanted something to do. She wanted to move on with her life.

My villa came into view. Warm lights lit up the inside and I smiled, knowing she was waiting for me. No more coming home to darkness. We could eat dinner, then I had plans to get her naked on the couch and make her come as many times as I could.

Yeah, I liked coming home to her.

I should never have stayed away from her, but maybe I hadn't been in the right place back then. Hadn't been the man she needed.

It didn't matter. Now, I was never letting her go.

I opened the front door and was hit by warmth and good smells. I smelled cinnamon from whatever candle she'd been burning. And there were some delicious smells coming from the kitchen.

I dumped my keys. Yep, I was looking forward to a quiet night, just the two of us.

I rounded the corner and stopped short.

Alessio was with Georgie at the stove, both of them stirring a pot. Bastian was sitting on a kitchen stool, a glass of wine in hand and an open bottle beside him. Landon was setting plates on the table and Cole was on the couch with a beer.

An undecorated Christmas tree sat by the window.

"What the hell are you guys doing here?"

Bastian smiled and lifted his glass at me. Georgie turned and grinned, happiness shining off her.

"Hey, the guys showed up and they brought a Christmas tree." She waved a hand. "A real live Christmas tree and a bunch of decorations for it. They decided to stay for dinner, and after, we can decorate."

My jaw worked. I just bet they'd decided to stay for dinner.

"Alessio is showing me a secret recipe for the best pasta sauce on the planet."

With her so happy she was glowing, I couldn't stay mad.

I walked over and gave her a kiss. When she went back to the stove, Bastian held out a beer to me. "You can have her to yourself later."

"Or you guys could find your own women."

"Too many beautiful fish in the sea."

"The table's all set." Landon announced. He accepted a glass of wine from Bastian.

Georgie clapped her hands together. "Excellent. Dinner is almost ready."

———

Sitting at the table, my belly full of some very good pasta, my arm around a snort laughing Georgie, I felt pretty damn good.

Landon was telling a funny story from the clinic.

"The guy ran out of the exam room, naked as a jaybird. Picture a six foot five inch Black man packed with muscle. Kids and women were screaming. It took me forever to catch him and sedate him."

I fiddled with Georgie's hair. Despite the change in plans, we'd had a good evening.

The food had been excellent, and the tree was now decorated. The guys probably wouldn't admit it, but they'd had as much fun decorating it as Georgie. The lights on it blinked merrily in red, green, and white.

I had good friends. They'd welcomed Georgie with open arms and gave her a sense of family.

"Georgie, how's your job hunt going?" Bastian asked.

Her nose wrinkled. It was cute and I wanted to kiss her.

"I haven't found anything right for me yet. It's hard since I don't have any experience. I might need to just start as a waitress or bartender for a while."

Yeah, that wasn't going to happen.

"With my degree in event planning, I'm sure Las Vegas will offer up the right opportunity. Eventually."

"There's no rush," I reminded her. "You can take your time."

"I can't sit around making candles all day," she huffed.

Bastian leaned back in his chair. "I have an early Christmas gift for you."

I scowled at him. "You can't give my woman Christmas gifts."

"Yes, I can." He looked back at Georgie. "Tomorrow, you have an interview. With the head of Events here at the Avernus."

Georgie sat up straighter, then pulled a face. "I won't take a pity job from you, Bastian."

"It's not that. It's an interview. A toe in the door. It's up to you to get the job. Now, I will put in a good word for you. I've seen your skills, your drive, your work ethic. It's an entry-level job working for Marilyn Strauss. She's been working in event planning for decades. I poached her from Caesar's Palace. I suspect the Army wishes they could recruit her. She runs everything with military precision and she doesn't suffer fools. She won't hire you if she doesn't think you can do it."

I saw excitement on my woman's face. She wanted the job.

"Really?" Georgie asked.

"Really." Bastian sipped his wine. "She's expecting you in her office tomorrow, ten o'clock. The rest is up to you."

Georgie bounced in the chair and clapped her hands. "Thank you!" She leaped up and threw her arms around Bastian.

I narrowed my eyes.

My asshole of a friend caught my gaze and took his time hugging my woman.

I'd kill him later. Right now, I was too pleased that he'd made my woman so happy.

CHAPTER 40
GEORGIE

olding tight to Nash's hand, we walked across the grass. At this time of year, it was lush and green. We circled a small man-made lake, surrounded by tall, straight palm trees. Dull gray clouds clogged the sky and there was a cold wind blowing.

Tomorrow was Christmas Day.

Just a few weeks ago, I hadn't been looking forward to the holiday. I'd been dreading it. I'd been too tangled up in my grief and need for revenge.

Now, I couldn't wait. I felt like a little kid again. I squeezed Nash's hand and he squeezed back. He was going to make breakfast for us, and we'd open our presents by the tree. Later, I was going to cook a turkey for a gang of retired assassins. My lips quirked.

If anyone had told me what I'd be doing at Christmas, I wouldn't have believed a single word. Wouldn't have believed that I'd be in love, happy, and with so many possibilities ahead of me.

Then I saw the marker set in the ground and my heart squeezed painfully.

I stared at the words inscribed on the gravestone.

Vivienne Linden.

Beloved daughter and sister.

Forever loved.

My throat tightened. I squeezed Nash's hand again, then crouched. I set the flowers I carried down beside Viv's gravestone.

"Hi, Viv." I touched the smooth stone. It was the first time I'd been here. "I just wanted to come and see you, but... You aren't here. You're free and flying high." I smiled, tears welling in my eyes. "With Elliot, and mom and dad." My chest hitched. "I miss you all so much, but you don't need to worry about me. I'm doing okay. And I'm not alone."

I stood, and Nash wrapped an arm around me. I leaned into him. He was wearing a brown leather jacket and looked so good.

"Nash is taking good care of me. Viv, I hope you're taking good care of yourself. I love you." I looked at the beautiful orchids that Nash had put together for me. They were gorgeous. Viv would've loved them.

"It's Christmas tomorrow. I'm making eggnog, but Nash bought me a bottle of really good pink champagne. I'll have some for you." I grinned. "I also got a new job! I interviewed with the most intimidating woman I've ever met. She's smart, experienced, and bossy. I'll be working in Events at the Avernus casino. Can you believe it?"

Sadness washed over me. God, I wished she was here. I could almost hear her squeals of excitement, her happy laughter.

"I promise I'll come back." My voice was thick. "I'll bring you some more of Nash's orchids, and I'll tell you all about the new job."

I talked a little longer, sharing everything new in my life with the sister I loved.

"Well, we'd better go."

Nash hugged me.

"My man has promised to teach me poker. I figured I can't live and work at a casino if I can't play poker." I swiped away the tears in my eyes. "Love you, Viv."

I let Nash lead me back to the Range Rover. As we walked, the clouds parted and a stream of sunlight hit us. Like a light shining down from above.

I laughed, happiness welling inside me. "That's got to be Viv. She always said there was no greater feeling than stepping into the spotlight."

My man smiled back. "I don't know, for me, there's no greater feeling than knowing you're standing right beside me."

———

I arched my hips up, crying out as my orgasm hit me hard. I came on Nash's face, my thighs clenching on his head.

With a growl, he kept licking me, working me through it. His hands slid under my bare ass, holding me in position.

Finally, I collapsed back on the rug under the Christmas tree, breathing heavily. My limbs felt warm and heavy.

He sat back on his knees, grinning, and wiped his forearm across his glistening mouth. "Merry Christmas, sweetheart."

I let out a husky laugh. It was Christmas morning. I was wearing my new, super cute red plaid Christmas pajama set with Merry and Bright written on the front of the shirt. Well, I was wearing half of the set. The tiny shorts were... I looked around. I had no idea where they were. Nash had stripped them and my panties off me in one swift move.

His hand skimmed up my leg. "I hope you enjoyed your first gift."

"I did. Very much." My gaze dropped to the hard cock tenting the front of his red pajama pants.

His low chuckle sent goosebumps over my bare skin. "You can have that gift later." He shifted, then passed me my missing panties and shorts.

While I shimmied into them, Nash poured us both a glass of eggnog. I sat cross-legged, excitement whizzing through me. I felt like I was ten years old again, bouncing with uncontained anticipation at the thought of opening all my gifts.

Nash sat beside me and I sipped the cinnamon-and-nutmeg goodness of the eggnog.

"Okay, first gift for you." He reached for a wrapped present under the tree.

"I already got my first gift."

His lips curled. "Fine, your second gift."

I tore the wrapping paper off and gasped. It was a stunning blue orchid with pink veins running through the petals. It was nestled in a pretty ceramic pot.

"Nash, it's so stunning. One of yours?"

He nodded.

"What's it called?"

"Forever Yours."

Love swamped me. I set the pot down and leaned over to kiss him. He tasted like Nash, eggnog, and love.

I sat back and pulled a large, wrapped box from under the tree. "Open it."

He carefully opened the wrapping paper. It was a set of orchid snips. "Georgie…"

"They're handmade in Japan. Damascus forged."

"I know." His hand reverently smoothed over the box. "I've wanted some for ages. They're expensive."

I blushed. "So you like them?"

"I love them."

My next present was a gift card to the stores at the Avernus.

"Now that you're working in the Events team, I figured you'd need some new work clothes."

I beamed at him.

"And if you splurge on some lingerie, your man won't complain one little bit." He winked.

I handed him his next gift. He opened the new, black leather wallet and cocked his head.

"I saw you still had the same wallet I gave you for your twenty-first birthday. It was falling apart."

"I love that wallet."

"Well, I confiscated it. And now you'll love this one. Open it."

He flicked the wallet open and the old photo of me was still inside. God, I'd been so young. So unaware at what life would throw at me. But I'd made it. I'd survived and hadn't let it beat me down.

Beside the photo was a new one. Of me and Nash. Bastian had taken it. I was smiling right at the camera. Nash was smiling too, but looking at me. I loved it.

He looked up. "Thank you."

"And I found a way to reuse the old wallet." I handed him his final gift and hoped he liked it.

He opened the small box and pulled out the masculine, braided leather wristband.

"I know you don't wear jewelry, and if you don't like it, you don't have to wear it. I found a guy here in Las Vegas who works with leather. He repurposed the leather from your old wallet into this."

Nash touched it, his finger flicking at the two silver beads worked into the band. One was inscribed with an N and the other a G.

"It's fucking perfect, Georgie." He slipped it onto his left wrist. "I'm never taking it off. Now come here and kiss me."

I crawled into his lap and soon the kiss was getting hot, heavy, and interesting.

He nipped my bottom lip. "I have one more present for you."

I wriggled my ass against his growing cock. "I know."

"Not that." He handed me one more small gift.

I opened it and uncovered a small box. I flicked it open and gasped. "Nash, it's beautiful. I've never seen anything like it."

The pendant was an oval-shaped jewel that glittered an amazing green-yellow color.

"It's a Montana sapphire," he said. "They're mined in Montana and known for their amazing colors, from blues, teals, greens, and oranges. I'd never heard of them, but I was looking for something to match your eyes. And when I found this bi-color sapphire, I knew I'd found it."

"I love it." I handed it to him. "Put it on." I turned away from him.

He put the necklace around my neck and fastened it. The unique sapphire was cool against my skin.

I smiled back at him. "Best Christmas ever."

"I'm damn glad you're back in my life, Georgie. I was

eating and breathing, but I wasn't living before. I was sleepwalking until I found you again."

Warmth filled me. God, I loved this man. "Don't make me cry."

He pushed a strand of hair behind my ear. "We should make breakfast. Knowing the guys, they'll be over here well before the time I told them they could come."

I bit back a smile at the grumpiness in his voice. "But you haven't given me my final gift and I want it."

His brow creased and he glanced at the base of the tree.

I slid my hand down and toyed with the waistband of his pajama pants. "I mean this big, thick gift right here that needs unwrapping."

He sucked in a breath.

I touched the tip of my tongue to my lip. "Then, it might need sucking."

With a growl, he tumbled me back into the pile of discarded wrapping paper. "What it needs is to be inside you." He kissed me. "You want it, sweetheart, it's all yours. Every part of me belongs to you."

CHAPTER 41
NASH

Two weeks later

I walked across the casino floor with Theo. We were discussing some security improvements.

"I think we should add two more security guards to the main floor."

Theo nodded. "Done. The new hires are shaping up nicely, so we won't have a problem with that."

We passed several blackjack tables. A pretty, young redheaded dealer had all her players laughing and smiling as she expertly dealt the cards.

The casino crowd was a little thin right now, since it was the afternoon. But in a few hours, I knew the place would fill up.

Then I saw my woman walking toward me and all thoughts left my head.

Beside me, Theo laughed. "I guess we've finished our work discussion."

Georgie wore a neat navy-blue suit. The long, fitted skirt hugged her body, a crisp white shirt was tucked into it and topped with a tailored jacket. The skirt alone ignited a few fantasies. Some naughty boss and employee ones that I'd enjoy playing with her later. I was gratified to note she'd put on a few pounds and was glowing with health and happiness.

"Hi," she said. "I just finished work."

"Me too."

Her lips quirked. "You were coming to find me, weren't you?"

"Yes." I dropped my head and kissed her. "How was your day?"

"Amazing." She snuggled into me. "Marilyn is a little scary, but I love it. She's very detail-oriented and expects everybody to keep up with her. We're planning a wedding for next weekend. It's going to be mind-blowing. I love my new job."

I could see that. And I'd heard from Bastian that Marilyn was thrilled with Georgie.

"I have my dream job and my dream man." Her smile dimmed. "I wish Viv was here to see it. And Elliot."

I pulled her close. "They can see it."

My thoughts turned to my best friend. *Buddy, I'll take good care of her. You were right, she's too sweet for me, but I swear, no one will love her as much as I do.*

I didn't get a response, but I liked to think he was happy for us.

"I'm sure there's some rule about staff members canoodling on the casino floor," a voice drawled.

Ignoring Bastian, I hauled Georgie off her feet and kissed her hard. When I broke the kiss, she was laughing.

Bastian stood beside us, watching us with a smile and a cocked eyebrow.

I set Georgie down. "I'm a consultant, not an employee."

"Semantics."

"I'm not going to stop kissing my woman. *Ever.*" I slid an arm around her.

"I'm going to order in dinner tonight," Bastian said. "Landon said he'll drop by. Alessio's away, and Cole's a maybe."

I figured Alessio was off on another side job. I glanced at Georgie and she nodded. "We're in. I'll bring—"

There was a blur of movement to my right. Suddenly, a small figure launched through the air and crashed into Bastian.

Georgie gasped and I yanked her backward, out of the line of fire.

There were shocked cries as people nearby scrambled out of the way.

Bastian didn't go down. He caught his attacker, but the added weight made him stagger.

That's when I realized his attacker was female. Hell, it was the female dealer with the red hair I'd seen earlier.

She moved like a damn acrobat, slipping up and wrapping her thighs around Bastian's neck.

As she twisted, this time he fell, trying to pull her off him.

They crashed to the carpet.

"Fuck," I muttered.

"Aren't you going to help him?" Georgie gasped, wide-eyed.

"No, he's got it."

Bastian yanked on the woman's red hair and the wig fell off. She was short, petite, with a fit body. Her dark hair reached her shoulders and complemented large, brown eyes.

"Lark, I—" Bastian started.

She flipped and pinned him to the floor. "Shut up. I'm just here to kill you."

Georgie sucked in a sharp breath.

I watched the tiny assassin pull a knife from under her vest. Bastian reared up and knocked it away.

She leaped off and launched a kick at him. He jerked to the side, and her booted foot narrowly missed his head.

I knew she was well-trained. There'd be enough power in that kick to incapacitate.

Bastian rose, his gaze locked on her. "Lark," he growled.

"You killed him, now I'll kill you." She drew another knife.

The way she held it showed she knew exactly how to use it.

She threw it.

Bastian moved like water—fast, liquid. The knife embedded in the blackjack table beside him.

He rushed her, but she leaped onto another table, scattering chips everywhere. People screamed. Another knife appeared in her hand.

Several security guards, including Theo, were closing in fast.

Lark clocked them and her face twisted, then she tossed the knife and leaped off the table.

Dammit. She landed in a crowd of people and disappeared. I scanned around, but there was no sign of her.

"Fucking hell," Bastian muttered.

"Oh no," Georgie cried.

He had a knife embedded in his right shoulder. He gripped the hilt and pulled it out.

"Are you okay?" Georgie hurried over to him.

Impatiently, Bastian yanked his tie off, wadded it into a ball, and pressed it to the bleeding wound. "I'll live."

I cleared my throat. "If she wanted to really kill you, you'd be dead."

"I know." A dark look settled on his face, his gaze on the spot where she'd disappeared.

"Who is she?"

"Lark," I said. "The woman who's always trying to kill him."

Georgie blinked. "No."

"Yes," Nash said.

Bastian sniffed. "I have no plans to be killed anytime soon." He impatiently studied his shoulder. "Raincheck on dinner?"

I nodded. "Bastian, you need to take care of her. This is the fourth time she's attacked you. Eventually, she will aim to kill."

A look that I couldn't decipher crossed his face. "I'll deal with her."

Georgie shifted Bastian's hand and checked his wound. "You need a doctor. This needs glue or stitches."

"I'll take care of it," Bastian said. "I'm more upset that she put a hole in my suit jacket. It's Armani."

Georgie rolled her eyes.

Now Bastian smiled. "Do you want to play nurse, Georgie?"

"Don't make me kill you," I muttered.

"I'll be fine. I'll get the hotel doctor to check it out." Then he spun and stalked off toward the elevators.

I took Georgie's hand and nodded at Theo. I knew he'd deal with things here.

"What was that all about?" Georgie demanded. "Will he be all right?"

"It's a long story. He'll be fine."

"She's an assassin?"

"Yes. Trained by Bastian's old mentor, Ed Galloway. The man practically raised Lark, and she thinks of him as a father."

"Okay. So why is she trying to kill Bastian?"

"Because Bastian killed Galloway. She blames him."

Georgie's eyes went wide.

"He had his reasons. And now, he and Lark are mortal enemies."

"He was trying not to hurt her," Georgie murmured.

"Yeah. She's the only person I know who knocks him off balance. She's deadly, but she hasn't actually killed him. He's protective of her. It's complicated."

"Hmm, well, I guess we'll see how it plays out." Georgie straightened. "But there's no way we're letting her kill him."

"Right." I pulled her outside and headed toward our villa. "How about we forget about Bastian and his problems and get home? I have a new orchid for you."

"You do?"

"It's yellow. I called it the Vivienne."

She shot me a sweet smile. "I love you."

"I know. And I've loved you for far longer than I ever knew. And I'll love you in this life, and the next."

———

I hope you enjoyed Georgie and Nash's story!

The Unsanctioned series continues with **No Matter the Cost**, starring casino owner Sebastian "Bastian" Thorne and assassin Lark. **Read on for a preview of the first chapter.**

Don't miss out! For updates about new releases, free books, and other fun stuff, sign up for my VIP mailing list and get your *free box set* containing three action-packed romances.

Visit here to get started: www.annahackett.com

Would you like a FREE BOX SET of my books?

PREVIEW: NO MATTER THE COST

BASTIAN

It looked like an ancient Egyptian temple.

I walked across the stage. The show was coming together well. The massive columns rising toward the ceiling looked like real stone, but I knew they were merely foam, expertly painted by the stage crew.

Lights clicked on, showcasing a large statue of the Ancient Egyptian god, Anubis, the jackal-headed god of funerary rites. I knew the special-effects team was still working out some kinks, but I could easily imagine the cast on stage, in their Egyptian costumes, telling the story of the god, Osiris, and his goddess wife, Isis.

It was a gripping tale of love, betrayal, and rebirth.

Yes, the Avernus Casino had a hit on its hands. The tourists would flock to see it.

My lips curved. *Perfect.* I enjoyed the challenge of running my casino. I also enjoyed making lots of money.

"We need to beef up security around the VIP seats," a deep voice said beside me.

I flicked a glance at my friend and security consultant, Nash Oakley. He was studying the auditorium seating, his arms crossed and a frown on his face.

"Agreed. We have a Saudi prince coming on opening night, along with several New York heiresses on a bachelorette party. Not to mention lots of local Las Vegas personalities."

Nash grunted. I knew he was working through the security plan in his head. "I'll coordinate with Theo."

Theo was head of security for the Avernus. The older former military man always got the job done.

"Excellent."

I saw Forrest, our eccentric costume designer, push a rack of clothes onto the stage. Several actors trotted along behind him, most of them already in costume.

"Come on, come on." The goateed man waved at them. "I need to see if everything works under the lights. There'll be adjustments that I need to make. Hurry up, now."

I saw the muscular Osiris—clad in a white skirt, a collar of gold and lapis lazuli draped over his chest and shoulders. His large headdress was the white crown of Upper Egypt, adorned with a golden cobra.

He was followed by the willowy Isis, wearing a gauzy, white dress, and a vulture headdress in brilliant gold.

It was a gripping story—the god Osiris killed by his jealous brother Set, who throws his body into the Nile. Osiris' wife, Isis, searches for him and brings him back to life with her magic, and they conceive their son, Horus. But Osiris' time on Earth is over, and he becomes the King of the Underworld.

I watched Forrest hover, tugging on hemlines, and fussing over crowns and headdresses. It was the perfect show for the Avernus. I felt a special affinity to the underworld.

As a former assassin, it felt right.

That's why I'd called my casino the Avernus, after a volcanic crater and lake in Italy that was rumored to be an entrance to the underworld in Roman mythology.

Nash was another former assassin. In fact, quite a few retired assassins called the Avernus home these days. My lips quirked. I seemed to have a knack for collecting battered souls.

I liked that the casino kept me busy. It was what I needed to stop from overthinking. I knew that the past was best left in the past, but sometimes, things best left in the dark liked to rear their heads. Still, I'd learned that regrets never helped, never changed the outcome.

I'd come from nothing, then been recruited into the CIA. I'd become the best assassin they'd ever created. Then, I'd faked my own death and started a new life.

Now, it was my choices, my way.

"By the way, I sent that report you requested to your email," Nash said. "On the Red Ribbon Killer."

I was careful not to stiffen. "Thank you."

"You going to tell me why you're interested in a noto-rious serial killer who's never been caught?"

"No."

Nash sighed. "Fine. So, do you have a plan for dealing with Lark?"

My muscles tensed at the change of subject. "I said I'd deal with her."

"Bastian, she's tried to kill you four times. You can't just ignore her."

My mouth flattened.

Nash sighed. "Look, I get it. You're connected through Ed. She was practically his daughter, and he treated you like a son."

Ed Galloway.

A gallon of conflicting emotions surged up inside me. Once, I'd believed he was the greatest man I'd ever known. A top CIA agent. A patriot. He'd been the one to recruit a cocky, homeless teenager. He was the one person who'd seen potential in me.

I'd been an abandoned baby, then a foster kid, then a runaway surviving on the street when Ed had changed my life.

And a few years later, he'd taken in a grieving, orphaned girl whose family had been massacred. He'd raised Lark as his own.

Nash was right. I'd considered Ed a father figure, like Lark did. Not that I'd ever felt anything brotherly toward her. My feelings for Lark were as complex as my ones for Ed.

But then everything had changed when I'd learned that the man I'd known all my life was a lie.

I blew out a breath. "I said I'll deal with her. When

you've made the security adjustments for opening night, let me know." I swiveled and strode out of the auditorium.

Back on the main floor of the casino, the jaunty songs of the slot machines and the familiar hubbub of gamblers at the tables filled my ears. The casino decor was black and bronze. The black carpet was shot through with geometric bronze designs. The servers and dealers all wore uniforms consisting of black pants and shirts, topped with bronze vests.

"I'm *not* going to let you ignore this," Nash said.

I spun to face him.

"You're my friend," he said. "You've saved my ass plenty of times. Had my back. I'm not keen to see her put a bullet in your brain."

"She won't."

He made an annoyed sound. "You sound so sure of that."

"She'd slit my throat, not shoot me."

His mouth flattened. "Bastian—"

That's when I felt it. The familiar prickle on the back of my neck. My finely-tuned senses detected someone watching me. I had really good instincts from growing up on the streets, but the CIA had sharpened them to a honed blade.

Lark was here.

I glanced up, not doing anything to give away that I knew she was present. I just lazily scanned the casino like I was going about my normal business.

There was no sign of the pint-sized assassin. I wasn't surprised. She was a master of disguise, and could blend in anywhere.

She'd attacked me right here on the casino floor last

week. I resisted the urge to reach up and rub the healing stab wound on my shoulder.

"Bastian?"

I met Nash's gaze. "I'll deal with her."

My friend nodded. Then his rugged face looked over my shoulder and changed. His lips moved into a smile.

I knew exactly what I'd see when I looked behind me. Or rather, who.

I turned. Yes, Georgie Linden—the newest member of the Avernus Events team—was walking toward us. She'd put on a little weight since she'd hooked up with Nash. Her gentle curves filled out her smart gray pantsuit and her blonde hair was up in a stylish twist.

She was the little sister of Nash's best friend from his childhood, and the love of his life.

She'd come to Las Vegas to save her sister from a predator. She'd failed, but with Nash's help, she'd gotten revenge and taken down the man who'd murdered her sister.

"Hello." Georgie smiled at Nash.

The man pulled her in close and kissed her. "Hi."

Georgie's blue eyes flicked my way. "Bastian, everything is coming together so well for the Isis and Osiris show. Ticket sales have gone through the roof since we launched the advertising campaign."

Excitement glowed off her.

"That's what I like to hear."

Nash snaked his arm around his woman. "Are you on your lunch break?"

"I am."

Like he had to ask. I knew the man had her timetable memorized.

"Good. Lunch is on me. Bye, Bastian." He herded her away.

She waved at me as they left.

I stood there, alone in the sea of people. For the first time, I felt a flash of envy watching them. I never lacked for female company when I wanted it, but I'd never had that…connection. Never had a woman look at me the way Georgie looked at Nash. Usually, they looked at me and saw a hard body or dollar signs.

I caught a flash of green out of the corner of my eye and turned my head.

It wasn't Lark. I felt a strange sense of disappointment.

A willowy blonde sauntered my way. She was putting a good deal of effort into the enticing sway of her hips.

"Hello." She shot me a slow smile. "You look lonely." She cocked her head. "I have a friend, Samantha. She's played with you before." The blonde lifted a hand and one red-tipped nail fiddled with a button on my shirt. "She said you rocked her world." The woman's voice turned breathy.

I leaned in and pulled in a breath of her musky perfume. She was my type, but for some reason I fought the urge to wrinkle my nose.

"Want to rock mine?" she asked.

I shot her my practiced smile. "Darling, I appreciate the offer, but I can't right now." The truth was, I only had the vaguest blip of attraction. My attention was elsewhere. I brushed her cheek with my fingers. "Rain check?"

Her plump lips curled. "Okay. I won't forget. Until next time."

She walked away with more of that swing in her hips. She was exactly the type that I partied with. I liked them tall, leggy, and simple. Women were just another pleasant diversion. I never let things get too complicated.

I had one rule. No repeats.

I walked toward the elevator that would lead to my office and penthouse. I couldn't sense Lark anymore and I bit back my frustration.

Where are you, little bird?

Then suddenly I stopped. A scent tickled my senses and I breathed deep, pulling in a lungful. It smelled of fresh rain and thunderstorms.

Lark.

She always smelled like a rainstorm.

She'd been here.

I turned in a slow circle, giving the floor one last scan. But I already knew she was long gone.

I needed to find her and do what I'd promised Nash that I would—deal with her.

Soon.

———

LARK

I fed coins into the slot machine, but my gaze was on *him*.

Sebastian "Bastian" Thorne.

A huge mess of emotions tangled inside me. I knew it wasn't the name he'd been born with, or the one he'd used when he was younger. He'd had a lot of names. I lifted my hand and rubbed a closed fist against my chest, pushing the emotions away.

I knew that trying to pull them apart just made me more confused and annoyed. I drew in a deep breath, then stabbed at the buttons on the machine. On the screens, icons spun and blinked.

Someone brushed past me.

"Sorry, ma'am," a man called out, paying me no attention.

I was dressed as a sixty-something woman. My hair was a curly, gray wig and I wore a billowy, patterned shirt, with boring, pastel-peach pants. I'd added padding around my hips to fill out my shape, and my platform sandals added a few inches of height.

I'd also used makeup putty to tweak my facial features and avoid the pesky facial-recognition system. There was a camera right above me, in fact. I knew exactly where all the cameras were in the Avernus Casino.

Bastian was talking with his friend, Nash Oakley. Another retired assassin. Oakley had been military, then black ops. They looked like they were having an intense conversation. A moment later, a woman joined them, and Nash wrapped his arm around her. I knew her name was Georgiana Linden. I had notes on everyone who was close to Bastian. After some more conversation, the couple left.

Bastian stood there, alone. He was so damn good-looking. I scowled. That annoyed me.

Today, he wore a dark-gray suit. Bespoke. I knew that he liked designer labels, so it was probably Armani or Brioni or some other tailor I'd never heard of. His white shirt looked good against his bronze skin. His thick, black hair was well styled, and he had a handsome face. Not quite classical, because it had too much of an edge, his features a little too hawkish. He wasn't pretty, but he definitely caught the eye.

Even with the face, and the coating of wealth and charm, I knew he was dangerous.

Then I stiffened. A woman in a clingy, green dress sauntered up to him.

Ugh. Her fake boobs were so obvious, and her long legs were slender without a single sign of any muscle tone. I could snap her like a twig, even though she was half a foot taller than me. She had a fall of artful curls that she'd dyed platinum blonde.

She was his type. Bastian seemed to like willowy, well-groomed, and temporary.

They spoke for a short time, then she left with a smile. But he'd smiled at her and touched her cheek. I gritted my teeth.

I had to kill him.

Anger flooded me. *There.* I liked that much better.

Bastian had killed my mentor.

Ed.

Grief was a hollow feeling. An emptiness.

I breathed through it. My parents had been murdered when I was ten. I barely remembered them now. I did remember that they'd locked me in a closet when our isolated cabin had been attacked. I'd heard the entire assault.

I'd heard them die.

My hands gripped the side of the slot machine. The images only came in bits and pieces. My entire existence before the age of ten was just faded and tarnished memories of another life.

Ed had saved me. The CIA agent had carried me from that blood-soaked cabin and given me a fresh start.

He'd trained me to fight, shoot, hunt, track. Every skill I'd needed to protect myself.

Every skill I'd needed to turn into the hunter, instead of the prey.

He'd molded me into an assassin, and he'd become my family.

Then, a year ago, I'd gone on a job. When I'd come back to visit Ed, I'd found him dead in his bed. A single gunshot wound between the eyes.

It had been an execution.

He'd been killed by the Reaper. The most fearsome assassin in the world. One people still whispered about, even though he was supposedly long gone.

He wasn't gone. He'd just changed his name to Bastian Thorne.

My next breath was ragged. He'd left me a note.

We need to talk

– B.

I hadn't wanted to talk. I still didn't want to talk. No, I'd raged and cried and screamed. What I wanted was revenge.

Ed had been my savior, my adopted father. Bastian had ended him.

I rose and walked closer to him. Almost close enough to touch. I kept my shoulders hunched, my walk slow, my gait uneven. The key to a good disguise wasn't just what you wore, but living and breathing it. Right now, I was an older woman with hip problems.

As I passed by him, my muscles twitched. I could attack him right now. I stared at his back. I could plunge my knife deep. I knew exactly where to hit for maximum impact.

A good assassin never acts on impulse.

That was Ed's voice.

One of his rules.

I kept walking, slow and steadily. I paused near a bar and glanced back.

Bastian was looking around. Like an impatient king surveying his domain.

How anyone believed that idiot Chance Tyler—the two-bit actor Bastian had hired to pretend to be the owner of Avernus—was the casino's owner was beyond me. You could see it was bullshit in an instant.

As I watched, Bastian disappeared into an elevator. I turned toward the exit of the casino.

I would kill Bastian.

I would take down my enemy.

I would have my vengeance.

But I wasn't a good assassin, I was a brilliant one. Ed had forged me into that.

I'd plan. I'd take my time.

I'd make the kill.

Bastian Thorne was a dead man walking.

———

BASTIAN

"Okay, that's the last event on the schedule," I said.

The man sitting on the other side of my desk crossed one leg over the other, studying the tablet in his hand. "Got it. It's good to be busy."

"There's a lot on this month, Chance, including the opening of the Isis and Osiris show. Be ready. If you have any questions, let me know."

The former actor nodded. His blond hair was perfectly styled and his teeth blinding white. He had an even tan, despite it being winter, which I knew was down to weekly appointments at his spa.

The assassin known as the Reaper had died, and no

one had ever known the abandoned runaway named Cameron. In my new life, I hadn't wanted my face plastered everywhere as the owner of the Avernus. Chance played that role for me, and I paid him very well in return.

I ran the business, and he attended the press conferences, the parties, the charity events, and the interviews. He hobnobbed with VIPs and high rollers.

That left me free to take care of business and do whatever the hell I wanted.

Chance tapped the tablet screen. "First up is the charity gala."

"Yes. You'll need a speech."

His gaze flicked my way. "You give away a lot of your fucking money, Bastian."

"Because I have a lot of it. And there are people who need it."

I'd started the Avernus with several bags of uncut diamonds I'd recovered on my very last kill for the CIA. They hadn't been mine. I hadn't earned them, but neither had the ruthless dictator I'd taken them from. I'd used them to build the casino, and from that investment, I could give back.

Chance grunted and rose. "Okay, I think that's everything. I'll catch you later."

I sank back in my leather chair, my gaze shifting to the view out the floor-to-ceiling windows. From here, I could see all of Las Vegas and the mountains in the distance.

I'd been born in Chicago, then abandoned at a fire station as a newborn. After several foster homes, I'd run away to take my chances on the streets.

Chicago had been fucking cold. I still hated the snow.

I liked Las Vegas better. I knew exactly what it felt like

to be alone and shivering, freezing cold, and worried if you'd survive the night.

As my gaze swept over the city below me, I wondered where Lark was. She had to be somewhere close.

Leaning forward, I opened the top drawer of my desk. I pulled out a small roll of black fabric and then opened it.

Inside lay a knife.

It was a beautiful blade, a piece of art. I picked it up. Lark had been forced to leave it when she'd last attacked me. I stroked the carbon steel. The knife was perfectly designed for an assassin with a no-glare finish and tough, sculpted hilt.

My office door opened, and Nash stepped inside. Smoothly, I slipped the knife away. He wasn't alone. He was followed by three other men.

"Did you forget how to knock?" I asked silkily.

Nash sat on the black-leather couch near the wall. "You keep ignoring me and this Lark situation. I brought in reinforcements."

I glanced at the others. The three men were all so different, but they had one thing in common. They were all former assassins.

They now all lived in villas on the golf course behind the casino and we'd become a messed-up family of sorts. The one closest to me was Cole Black. Broad, muscular, with a powerful body, you could tell in an instant that he was a brawler. He did very well for himself in the underground fight rings. He'd been a mercenary for a while, then a freelance hitman people had known as Darkwolf.

Landon Bradshaw stood beside him. He had smooth, dark skin, short hair the color of ink, and a dark goatee. Once he'd been the assassin known as the Blade. He'd been black ops like Nash. Now he was a doctor, and vowed only to use his skills to heal, not kill.

The final man moved silently across my office. Toward the windows. Alessio Rossi was lean, bronze-skinned, and covered in tattoos. The ex-mafia enforcer didn't say much, but he was always hypervigilant. He missed nothing.

"So, this is an intervention?" I asked.

"She *will* kill you," Nash said.

I sighed, sensing my friend's frustration. "She blames me for killing Ed. I haven't had the chance to explain to her why."

I'd had no choice but to kill him.

Lark blamed me, but didn't know the full story. I should have found a way to tell her, but hell, a part of me didn't want to ruin how she saw the only father she'd ever had.

"So you want to talk with her?" Landon asked in his smooth voice.

I resisted the urge to run a hand through my hair. "I owe her an explanation."

"It's been months since you took out Ed." Cole sat on a chair in front of my desk. "Why haven't you done it already?"

"Because he knows it will hurt her," Alessio said quietly. "She will learn that her father figure was a murderer. That he killed for fun."

And there it was.

I'd discovered Ed's sick secret. He'd been a fucking serial killer. He wasn't the honorable agent, the sanctioned assassin, the man who killed for his country. He was just another twisted, sick fuck who'd killed loving families. Who killed kids.

I hadn't told my friends all the details of Ed's depravity. I'd just given them a brief overview of my reasons for killing him.

Now, I slid a hand through my hair, trying to ignore the twist in my gut. "Lark hasn't exactly been receptive to talking. And yes, she'll be devastated."

Lark was a woman who'd already had enough devastation in her life.

"She's already grieving his death," Landon said. "She needs to know the truth."

I nodded. I couldn't avoid it any longer. "I'll talk to her."

Nash rose, his hands on his hips. "How are you going to do that without her putting a bullet in you, or stabbing you—again?" He shot a pointed look at my shoulder.

I resisted rubbing the wound on my shoulder. Lark had left a knife embedded in it. It was probably not the time to tell Nash that I'd kept the custom blade, cleaned it, and sometimes took it out to look at when I was alone.

"You can't get rid of me that easily." I smiled. "Besides, your lovely Georgie would miss me." I couldn't resist needling him.

Nash scowled.

"Has anyone heard from Rafe?" Cole asked.

Rafe Archer was the last member of our unconventional, retired-assassins group.

"He messaged," I told them. "He's still in Europe. He'll be back soon."

"He's on a job?" Landon asked.

"No idea." Rafe had been an assassin for MI6. A real-life James Bond. He was also very British and had a thing about privacy. Half the time, he never told us where he was going.

"He's probably buying some painting or statue," Nash said.

Rafe was an art connoisseur. His villa looked like a freaking gallery.

I looked at my watch. It was mid-afternoon. I tapped my fingers on the desk. My friends were right. I needed to find Lark.

My best bet was to let her find me.

Yes. If I lured her out, she'd come.

I'd be the bait.

Unsanctioned
Burn the World Down
No Matter the Cost
Also Available as Audiobooks!

PREVIEW: FURY BROTHERS

Want more action-packed romance? Then check out the **Fury Brothers**, starting with *Fury*.

I'm not looking for a hero, and definitely not a fake relationship with my new boss, nightclub owner Dante Fury—over six feet of dark, hot, and dangerous.

But he isn't taking no for an answer.

The plan was to run, live under the radar, survive. My life's been destroyed by some very bad people and everything I know is gone—career, friends, family. I thought I could hide as a bartender at New Orleans' hottest new club, Ember.

I can't trust anyone, but after I'm attacked, Dante is determined to play protector by claiming me as his. No one would dare touch the woman of one of the Fury brothers. Suddenly, I'm living at his place, and he's touching me, kissing me, taking care of me...

Dante makes it very hard to remember this relationship isn't real. He makes my heart race, but he's way out of my league, and he's protecting his own broken pieces.

Nothing this fake should feel this right.

The bad guys won't give up, but I'm starting to think the biggest danger to me is Dante Fury.

Fury Brothers
Fury

Keep

Burn

Take

Claim

Also Available as Audiobooks!

PREVIEW: LANGSTON HOTELS

Want more action-packed romance? Then check out **Langston Hotels.**

Attending the charity masquerade ball was my chance to let loose for one night. And as soon as I see him, I let the handsome stranger show me the hottest night of my life.

Except then I learn he isn't a stranger.

He's my new boss.

Tessa

I'm Windward born and bred. I love my family, my town, and my dream job managing my hotel. But now we've been bought by Langston Hotels. Cue stress and panic.

I'll do anything to make sure they don't ruin the charm and turn my hotel into a slick, modern, soulless shell.

What I wasn't counting on was jet-setting hotelier Ambrose Langston. Handsome, bossy, with a wide workaholic streak.

It doesn't take me long to realize he's also the man I let do very wicked things to me.

Ro

Transforming the Windward Resort is next on my plan. I'm on a mission to make Langston Hotels thrive and rub my father's face in it.

What I never expected was the locals of Windward being less than happy with my acquisition. And I definitely wasn't expecting Tessa Ashford.

I've always been professional with my employees, unlike my philandering father, but smart, beautiful Tessa —the mysterious woman who rocked my world—makes it a challenge.

Working side by side, all I can think about is her. I never stay. I work, then leave. But she has me questioning everything.

Then the strange "accidents" start happening. Someone doesn't want me in Windward.

Now, I need to keep Tessa safe from whoever wants me gone.

Langston Hotels

Night and Day

Before and After

Also Available as Audiobooks!

ALSO BY ANNA HACKETT

Unsanctioned

Burn the World Down

No Matter the Cost

Also Available as Audiobooks!

Langston Hotels

Night and Day

Before and After

Also Available as Audiobooks!

Hunter Squad

Jameson

North

Also Available as Audiobooks!

Fury Brothers

Fury

Keep

Burn

Take

Claim

Also Available as Audiobooks!

Unbroken Heroes

The Hero She Needs

The Hero She Wants

The Hero She Craves

The Hero She Deserves

The Hero She Loves

Also Available as Audiobooks!

Sentinel Security

Wolf

Hades

Striker

Steel

Excalibur

Hex

Stone

Also Available as Audiobooks!

Norcross Security

The Investigator

The Troubleshooter

The Specialist

The Bodyguard

The Hacker

The Powerbroker

The Detective

The Medic

The Protector

Mr. & Mrs. Norcross

Saving Mr. Norcross

Also Available as Audiobooks!

Billionaire Heists

Stealing from Mr. Rich

Blackmailing Mr. Bossman

Hacking Mr. CEO

Also Available as Audiobooks!

Team 52

Mission: Her Protection

Mission: Her Rescue

Mission: Her Security

Mission: Her Defense

Mission: Her Safety

Mission: Her Freedom

Mission: Her Shield

Mission: Her Justice

Also Available as Audiobooks!

Treasure Hunter Security

Undiscovered

Uncharted

Unexplored

Unfathomed

Untraveled

Unmapped

Unidentified

Undetected

Also Available as Audiobooks!

Oronis Knights

Knightmaster

Knighthunter

Galactic Kings

Overlord

Emperor

Captain of the Guard

Conqueror

Also Available as Audiobooks!

Eon Warriors

Edge of Eon

Touch of Eon

Heart of Eon

Kiss of Eon

Mark of Eon

Claim of Eon

Storm of Eon

Soul of Eon

King of Eon

Also Available as Audiobooks!

Galactic Gladiators: House of Rone

Sentinel

Defender

Centurion

Paladin

Guard

Weapons Master

Also Available as Audiobooks!

Galactic Gladiators

Gladiator

Warrior

Hero

Protector

Champion

Barbarian

Beast

Rogue

Guardian

Cyborg

Imperator

Hunter

Also Available as Audiobooks!

Hell Squad

Marcus

Cruz

Gabe

Reed

Roth

Noah

Shaw

Holmes

Niko

Finn

Devlin

Theron

Hemi

Ash

Levi

Manu

Griff

Dom

Survivors

Tane

Also Available as Audiobooks!

The Anomaly Series

Time Thief

Mind Raider

Soul Stealer

Salvation

Anomaly Series Box Set

The Phoenix Adventures

Among Galactic Ruins

At Star's End

In the Devil's Nebula

On a Rogue Planet

Beneath a Trojan Moon

Beyond Galaxy's Edge

On a Cyborg Planet

Return to Dark Earth

On a Barbarian World

Lost in Barbarian Space

Through Uncharted Space

Crashed on an Ice World

Perma Series

Winter Fusion

A Galactic Holiday

Warriors of the Wind

Tempest

Storm & Seduction

Fury & Darkness

Standalone Titles

Savage Dragon

Hunter's Surrender

One Night with the Wolf

For more information visit www.annahackett.com

ABOUT THE AUTHOR

I'm a USA Today bestselling romance author who's passionate about *fast-paced, emotion-filled* contemporary romantic suspense and science fiction romance. I love writing about people overcoming unbeatable odds and achieving seemingly impossible goals. I like to believe it's possible for all of us to do the same.

I live in Australia with my own personal hero and two very busy, always-on-the-move sons.

For release dates, behind-the-scenes info, free books, and other fun stuff, sign up for the latest news here:

Website: www.annahackett.com

www.ingramcontent.com/pod-product-compliance
Lightning Source LLC
Chambersburg PA
CBHW050354260626
47156CB00003B/722